The Dog Barked Murder:

The Curious Librarian
Cozy Mystery #3

A Novel By

Zana Hart

East Baton Rouge Parish Library
Baton Rouge, Louisiana

COPYRIGHT © 2015 Hartworks, Inc., PO Box 632, Crestone, CO 81131.

All rights reserved. This book or any portion thereof may not be reproduced or used in any manner whatsoever without the express written permission of the publisher except for the use of brief quotations in a book review.

This is a work of fiction. There are a few similarities to real life, based largely on the author's career as a librarian, but they are disguised.

Silvermine is a fictitious small town in Colorado, bearing similarities to Salida and Alamosa.

Cover photos of librarian and dog by Kelly Hart. The librarian is an actual library director. Cover design by Zana and Kelly Hart.

ISBN-13: 978-1514103173

ISBN-10: 1514103176

Table of Contents

ONE 1
TWO 6
THREE 10
FOUR 15
FIVE 20
SIX 26
SEVEN 31
EIGHT 38
NINE 44
TEN 47
ELEVEN 52
TWELVE 57
THIRTEEN 62
FOURTEEN 67
FIFTEEN 72
SIXTEEN 77
SEVENTEEN 82
EIGHTEEN 86
NINETEEN 91
TWENTY 97
TWENTY-ONE 102
TWENTY-TWO 106
TWENTY-THREE 111
TWENTY-FOUR 116
TWENTY-FIVE 121
TWENTY-SIX 126
TWENTY-SEVEN 132
TWENTY-EIGHT 137
TWENTY-NINE 144
THIRTY 150
A NOTE FROM THE AUTHOR 152

ONE

LAUREN LONG WALKED home from the Silvermine Public Library in the golden light of a June evening, glad to leave work behind for a couple of days. Spring came late in Colorado, but it was finally here and Lauren was ready to enjoy every minute of it. She would spend the weekend getting her house ready for Justin's return. He had been working for the Forest Service out of town for over a year, but now he would begin working from home as a consultant.

As she approached the house, she expected to see Mickey at the front window of her living room, in his regular spot. Usually he was barking eagerly, but this evening he wasn't in sight. Lauren hurried in and called him.

The house was unnaturally quiet. Mickey didn't come. Usually he would be jumping up on her by now. Her heart thumping, Lauren went out back to see if he had gotten stuck in the greenhouse that she and Justin had added to the back of the house. No, the dog door was fine.

She heard a soft noise in her bedroom and dashed in there, calling his name.

Mickey whined under her bed. She sat down on the floor next to the bed, and he met her eyes. Slowly he crawled out, into her lap, trembling and licking her hands obsessively.

She ran her hands over his little body, but there was no sign of any injury. When she stood up, he whimpered again. She picked him up and held him close to her chest. She was reminded of when she brought him home from the shelter in Denver. One of her brothers was driving, the dog was in her lap, and he trembled for the whole trip back to her family's

Aurora apartment. He had also been shaking when she drove over the mountains to Silvermine with him when she got the job as library director, just the two of them in her little car, his crate in the front passenger seat where they could see each other.

That had been over three years ago and now he was trembling just as badly again. What could have scared him so much while she was at work? Usually he was happy to see her and full of energy when she got back. He had accepted Justin in the house and was normally as happy to see Justin as to see her.

Best to walk across the street to Momo's house and get her advice. No time to change out of her work clothes, but none of her clothing would be harmed by dog hair. As Lauren walked with Mickey towards the front door, his trembling became more pronounced and he struggled to get out of her arms. So whatever scared him had been out front. She carried him out the back door from the kitchen, into the greenhouse and out into the backyard. It smelled of the sweet spring scent of lilacs. At least Mickey didn't seem to be injured, nor was he as frightened here.

As she stepped out the gate from her backyard, Mickey burrowed down even more into her arms. Momo lived across the street and down one house, and Arnold's pickup was in the driveway. Lauren smiled to think of the boomer romance between those two. They were about to take off for Mexico in the truck, going to the art town of Ajijic, where Momo was to have a show. Friends who lived there had arranged the show, thinking that Momo's visionary art would sell well to expats and Mexicans alike.

Lauren walked in the front door, calling out her hello.

Arnold looked up as he carried a couple of paintings toward the door. "Hi Lauren, how's it going? I thought we'd be down the road by now, but packing all these paintings is a big job. Momo is very particular about how each painting is handled," he said with a smile.

"Hey Arnold, I'm glad you two are still here. When I got home, Mickey was hiding under the bed. What's been going on in the neighborhood?"

Arnold automatically paid attention to things around him, because of his background as a state trooper. "There was a loud argument next door, you know the renters in the house directly across the street from you. Maybe that's what scared Mickey. It was over an hour ago."

He reached out his arms and Mickey let himself be transferred into Arnold's big embrace. With his rugged jaw, black hair turning gray, and strong arms, Arnold retained the good looks he'd obviously had as a younger man. Momo joined them from her painting studio, her silver hair disheveled and her painting apron covering dusty work clothes. "Hi dear," she said to Lauren. "What was Mickey bothered by?"

"You're the psychic one," Lauren said. "I came over to ask you. I worked a little late and just now got home."

"Well let's ask Mickey what happened," Momo said. She remained quiet while looking intently at the little dog. Mickey was content in Arnold's arms, basking in the attention they were all giving him. As Lauren tried to get a sense of what Mickey might be communicating, she regretted that her own intuitive powers were virtually non-existent. Momo had been psychic from childhood, and she seemed to think other people should pick up the skill easily. Lauren had been trying but without much luck.

"He says that the people across the street from you scared him," Momo began. "He was at the window watching for you, even though he knew you wouldn't be there yet. It still makes him feel good to be watching for you. Mike was yelling in his house, and Mickey is kind of used to that, he's heard it before. But then Tammi screamed. Mickey wanted to run across the street and sink his teeth into Mike's leg. He wanted to protect Tammi."

Momo looked at Arnold and said, "Did you hear all that going on?"

"Yes," he said. "I didn't hear anything that alarmed me, though. My antenna would have been out automatically for a really serious scream. But you know, there are the screams that matter and there are light-hearted screams. Mickey might not be as used to the difference as I am." Arnold and his wife had raised four girls, so he'd had plenty of chances to evaluate screams at close range.

"Let's see if Mickey has anything else to share," Momo said. "Yes, he's showing me a man he didn't like, out on the sidewalk on this side of the street. Mickey started barking at him from your living room, on the back of the recliner where he sits to supervise the street. The guy crossed the street, ran up through your little front yard and onto your porch. He looked down at Mickey though the window. The man made a loud growl while staring straight at Mickey, then he left and went on down the street. Mickey was so scared that he went and hid under the bed, even though he heard the man leave."

"Which event came first?" Lauren asked.

"They happened in the order he described, but he's not showing me whether there was much time between them. I think it happened when I was downtown running errands," Momo said. She added, "I know you can take care of yourself. You have certainly proved that more than once since you came to Silvermine. But if you need any psychic help while I'm in Mexico, be sure to check in with Betty. She inherited my natural abilities and she is working on using them when there's a need, rather than just whenever they turn up like they did that time when she was in high school."

"Yeah, you know we get together most weeks for family potlucks, and when Justin gets home I'm sure we'll do it more. She is always willing to help me out and I like to do a little babysitting with Rosie now and then. She loves for me to read her simple picture books, and she's gotten to where Betty and Don can go out and Rosie is happy enough with me. I go over to Betty's garden a lot now, to pick salad greens."

Betty was Momo's granddaughter, and she was married to Justin's younger brother Don. Lauren loved that the relationships made Momo some kind of kin to her.

Momo said, "I picked up takeouts from that Cambodian place. Why don't you and Mickey come back over here in half an hour? Do you have enough greens to make a salad?"

"Sure do, I'll whip one out and be back soon," Lauren said, retrieving Mickey from Arnold's embrace.

TWO

When they settled down to eat in Momo's kitchen, the truck was packed. Momo now looked immaculate, with her hair up, wearing beige jeans with a matching jacket, turquoise blouse, and informal turquoise jewelry. Arnold had spruced up too; his jeans and shirt were clean. Lauren noticed that they showed off his trim body nicely. Arnold liked his beer but he didn't let himself go to the point of having a belly.

"I bet you'll have a great time. I'm a little jealous," Lauren said. "It's been years since I've been to Mexico, and that was just to a couple of border towns when I was in college."

"I haven't been to Mexico for years either, and Arnold has never been." Momo dished up the Asian food as she spoke. "But now that Arnold and I are together, that art show invitation seemed like a great excuse to go have some fun. We're told that the violence in Mexico is played up in our press, and with Arnold along—and going in caravan with friends of his from Texas—I'm sure we'll be fine. Of course, I tuned in before deciding, and it all feels good."

Lauren reached down and scratched Mickey's ears. He was on the cushion that Momo kept under the table for him, dozing but with an ear cocked for the sound of any food falling. "I still wonder why Mickey was so upset. Do you think it was the neighbors arguing?"

Arnold said, "I'd bet it was the guy intruding on your porch that really got to him. I've known your neighbor Mike since he was a kid. He can be loud, but I don't think he's dangerous. I lived near Mike's parents, you know, over by the Episcopal church. I remember when Mike went in the Navy and when he got out of the service. He sometimes came over and chatted with us. Well, more with my wife. He has always had an eye for the ladies and she was a looker."

Lauren glanced at Momo, a beauty herself, and said to Arnold, "So you have an eye for the lookers too?"

Arnold said, "I can't deny it, and quite a few attractive women turned up after my wife passed away. I guess I needed some time, because Momo was the one who eventually caught my eye."

Momo almost choked on her food. "Caught your eye, my foot. Don't forget that we'd been friends for over twenty years." She pointed to Lauren with a smile. "But Lauren probably remembers how pleased I was after the first night that you spent here last year."

Lauren laughed. "Before you lovebirds take off on your adventure, is there any more background you want to give me on my loud neighbors? I don't know their whole story, just bits and pieces."

Arnold turned serious. "I don't think people realize how ambitious Mike is. He wants the so-called good things in life, and he is willing to do what it takes to get them. You know, Mike is really a control freak and he's that way with dogs as well as with people. That wife of his, Tammi, is part of his plan as I see it. She's good-looking, she's super sweet, and she makes a good teammate for their dog training business. Tammi being from out of town helps business too... she doesn't know people's histories. I expect they'll be good neighbors to you, Lauren, and I expect it will be calculated on Mike's part."

"Thanks, Arnold. They have both been friendly enough in the couple of months they've been renting the house, and he made sure to tell me it would be rare that they'd have noisy dogs at their house. I was embarrassed about that, since Mickey barks at Mike every chance he gets."

Lauren got up and cleared the table. "You two go on now and hit the road. I'll clean up your kitchen, Momo. And I'll tell the rest of the family that I've got your key, in case they need to go in for something."

"Speaking of family, how soon do you think you and Justin will get married?" Momo asked.

"I want to live with him for a while again and be sure we both want the commitment. Even though neither one of us wants to have kids, we still only want to get married if we're pretty sure it will really last. Then we'll see. Maybe next year. But I'll check before we set the date to see if you both will be in town. We're thinking of having a small ceremony at church, and then we'll have a huge party and potluck out on the land."

Arnold chuckled. "For a couple of kids who aren't sure if they want to get married, you've already got a lot planned about that wedding." He got up and began methodically checking through the house, being sure the windows were locked and that they hadn't left anything behind.

As she watched the boomers drive away, Lauren's eyes got misty. They were so dear together, and they had both been through so much. Arnold's wife had died a few years earlier, after a long bout with cancer, and Momo's husband had passed away when she was quite young. Momo had raised her daughter and developed her painting career in this house. Lauren hoped that Momo and Arnold would have the many years of happiness together that they deserved. But life didn't always seem to reward the deserving.

At home, Lauren and Mickey stretched out on the sofa. Their dog trainer, Samantha, was going to stop by later, after going bowling with Tammi, so maybe Lauren would hear more then about whatever had gone on across the street. In the meantime, she would continue reading the Agatha Christie novel she'd started on her lunch hour. She loved how Hercule Poirot considered details that everyone else thought were insignificant.

Mickey followed her everywhere, including into the bathroom. He often did, but tonight he was extra clingy. He barked just as she was starting to read. She glanced up from the sofa to see a car across the street. Tammi was leaving her house with Samantha and Jane, a dog rescuer and friend of

Sam's. They were all on a bowling team together. Sam had invited Lauren to join them this evening, but Lauren had thought she might be working late at the library. Good thing she was staying home, what with Mickey so upset. Hearing the voices through the open front windows, he retreated into the bedroom. Once the car left, he came back out and settled down again with Lauren on the sofa. "Maybe it's partly something about Tammi that scared you?" she asked him, but she didn't feel any kind of answer. Not that she had expected to.

Lauren loved how engrossing Agatha Christie novels were. She absorbed all the details and tried to second-guess what were real clues and what would turn out to be red herrings. A little later, when someone else came out of Mike and Tammi's house, she hardly noticed. But Mickey did. He went over to the front window and watched. That got Lauren's attention, and she saw an older man walk a little ways down the street to a white car and drive off in it.

She wondered what Hercule Poirot would have noticed in the scene. The man was wearing a striped business-style shirt. He had jeans on, though, not dress slacks. Was there anything remarkable about the clothing or the laptop he'd been carrying? Lauren thought not. The guy seemed totally ordinary. He'd been whistling a tune as he walked down the street. Lauren couldn't recognize the title at first but knew it was something her parents had listened to, maybe an old Louis Armstrong number. It was something upbeat. Oh, it was *What a Wonderful World.*

THREE

LAUREN RETURNED TO what Hercule Poirot was doing in the novel, but her concentration was shot. She wondered why Mickey had gone to hide at the sound of one car but not at the other one. Mike and Tammi did have a lot of visitors, mostly dog owners. The couple didn't have any dogs of their own, but they often brought boarding dogs home. Lauren had passed one or the other of them walking a dog along the sidewalk at different times, training the dogs for good manners. Tammi was easy-going, but Lauren remembered what Arnold had said about Mike being ambitious. He certainly wanted every dog she'd seen with him to be under his total control. Lauren had wanted to say to him, "Chill out," but she knew it would do no good. Besides, she wouldn't want a library patron telling her that at work. Sometimes Grace Johnson, the other librarian, did tell her to chill out, but only when Lauren was working too obsessively and needed a reminder.

Back to the novel. Lauren liked the setting, in a charming English town. It would be fun to go to England sometime with Justin. How about for their honeymoon? Mickey dozed beside her. How glad she was to have found him at the shelter. Part Sheltie and part Papillion, he was said to have come from a puppy mill and to have passed through Craigslist two or three times before the shelter got him. He was about five years old now and despite being high strung, he was gradually settling into a relatively peaceful life with her. But today was a setback. What was that trembling and hiding all about? Whatever it was, she would do her best to help him feel safer. He was such a dear little companion, and smart too. Finally, she absorbed herself in the plot and time passed without her being aware of it.

When Mickey started another barking binge, Lauren glanced up but saw no car out there. She stayed engrossed in her novel. Later, Mickey barked one sharp bark when a car stopped out front. A little reluctantly, Lauren put down the novel and saw it was Sam's car. She went to put the tea kettle on. It wasn't just Sam coming over; Sam's friend Jane was along, and it looked like Tammi was coming too. No, Tammi was going in her own front door. But even before the others got to Lauren's front door, Tammi was back with them. As they all came inside and greeted Lauren, Tammi was saying that Mike must have gone over to the Dog Place to take care of something. "So I'll see him later. That's kind of a relief. I expect he'll be back soon."

Sam said to Tammi, "Seems like he keeps you on a tight leash."

Tammi blushed through her makeup. "Oh, not really. I mean, I don't really mind. He takes everything so seriously."

Lauren described coming home to finding Mickey scared and asked Tammi if she knew what that could have been.

Tammi looked a little startled. "I don't think I was home," she said. "I was out getting groceries for a while."

Lauren had the feeling Tammi was lying. She wondered to herself how a woman had been screaming in the house if Tammi wasn't there. Her imagination, hyperactive after an hour with Agatha Christie, went wild momentarily. She reined it in, but she did notice that Mickey was avoiding Tammi. As the women brought their cups of tea into the living room, Lauren put out some nuts and dried fruit. Mickey fixated on the nuts, watching for someone to drop one.

They chatted about this and that, mostly bowling and dogs. Suddenly, Tammi got up.

"Please excuse me, but I think I'd better go on home. Thanks so much for everything, gals." Mickey watched her intently as she opened the front door. He climbed on the back of the recliner to watch her go across the street and enter her own house.

The conversation became livelier without her there. "Geez, she lets that guy walk all over her," Sam said. "She admitted to us this evening that he pushes her around. You wouldn't catch me putting up with that."

Sam didn't have boyfriends. She seemed to have few men in her personal life, though she was friendly with Justin whenever they met. But then they probably went to high school together. Would Lauren ever get used to all the interconnections in this small town? Having grown up around Denver, Lauren had romanticized small-town life when she first got the job here. The romanticism had worn off, but Lauren still loved Silvermine.

Mickey was still at the front window and he went into a frenzy of barking. "See how nuts he gets, Sam?" Lauren said. "When he's like that, I just can't get his attention."

Sam spoke with the natural authority of an expert. "Something else has his attention. Did either of you notice anything?"

They heard a scream. It had to be Tammi.

Mickey stopped barking and ran to the bedroom. Lauren was torn between getting him and going to see what had happened. That scream could have been serious, so she joined Sam and Jane as they hurried across the street. Sam knocked on the front door, with a firm loud knock, but she didn't wait for an answer before opening the door. Tammi was leaning over the kitchen floor. Mike lay there, with blood on his head... on his forehead and in his hair.

"Call 911," Tammi said. She made a long loud noise, not quite a scream.

"I'm going to check on Mike. One of you call 911," Sam said. Lauren's eyes fell on something lying across Mike's body. It was a dog leash, pink leather studded with fake rhinestones.

Jane called 911 on her cellphone. Then she squatted down and took a look at him as she said, "Look, I'm really sorry and I know this is weird, but I have to go. I promised Billy I'd get home to be with the kids." Nobody paid her much attention as she walked out. It crossed Lauren's mind to wonder how Jane was going to get home without a car, but it was the least of her concerns. Jane would take care of herself. What an odd moment to leave, though, Lauren thought.

Mike was lying on the kitchen floor, between the sink and the island. Sam checked his pulse and shook her head. Still, she began doing CPR on him. Lauren kneeled down and joined Sam in the rhythm, glad she'd had to take a CPR class for her job. She'd never done it before but Sam obviously knew what she was doing.

"He always worried about his heart," Tammi said through tears.

"This will be one for the police," Lauren said. Tammi gasped.

Lauren warned Tammi not to touch anything. "We need to be sure that any fingerprints can be taken. Just sit till the ambulance comes."

Like a child, Tammi took Lauren's advice, sitting on the floor next to them. "It wasn't the best marriage, he could be difficult, but I never wanted him to go," Tammi said. Sam glanced up at that comment, and she and Lauren exchanged a glance.

"I hear the siren a ways away," Lauren said. When the ambulance and police car arrived, an EMT took one look at Mike and told his colleague they'd better move fast. They loaded Mike quickly for the ride to the hospital. Lauren didn't see the dog leash when they took him out, but everything was happening so quickly. Tammi went to the hospital with Mike, in the ambulance.

"Lauren, you again?" Paul Johnson, the police officer, said in mock surprise. His wife Grace worked with Lauren at the library, and Paul knew about the times that Lauren had been involved in sleuthing mysterious deaths.

"Paul, you know perfectly well that I live right across the street from this house," Lauren said. "I have absolutely no interest in dealing with another mysterious death. I'll leave this alone, but be sure and check out that pink leash."

"What pink leash?" he asked.

"It was right here, draped across Mike," Lauren said. She heard how shaky her voice was. She would never get used to sudden death. "Well, if the leash disappeared, that's got to be a clue of some sort right there."

"Thanks Lauren," Paul said. "Just tell us what to look for any time you want to." His wry smile showed that he was teasing. Lauren commented that the way Mike's head looked to her, it had to be caused by someone. She didn't see how he could have gotten that blow just by falling in the kitchen. Paul nodded that he'd heard her. Lauren thought he was a really good police officer. He and Grace were black and had left Washington, D. C., to raise their kids in a calmer environment.

The rest of the evening passed in a blur. A police investigator evidently checked in with the hospital before coming to the house, and he told Paul that Mike had been dead on arrival. He and Paul took statements from Sam and Lauren and took Jane's phone number to contact her for a statement as well.

Sam said she would go by the hospital and see if she could do anything for Tammi. Lauren went home and went to bed with Mickey by her side. She felt shaken and had no impulse to read Agatha Christie.

FOUR

LAUREN SLEPT POORLY, but Mickey was a comfort, curled up on the bed with her. In the morning, she tried to think about ordinary things, like housework. She took a number of plants out of the greenhouse and got them in the ground in her backyard. But inevitably, her mind kept going back to what had happened. She thought of checking on Tammi but didn't want to go over too early.

In mid-morning, she heard a pounding on her front door. It was Tammi. While she went to the door, Mickey ran away from it. She guessed he was heading back under the bed.

"Lauren, can you help me? The police think I killed Mike. Well they didn't say so exactly, but when I went to the police station just now for an interview, they sounded suspicious." Tammi looked as frantic as her knocking had been.

Lauren took a deep breath. She thought that statistically the odds were pretty high that a wife would have done it. But she didn't say that to Tammi. "And you didn't kill him?" she asked.

"No, of course not! He's my husband, I mean, he was. I loved him, until... Well, I still love him. He's no saint but neither am I."

Lauren left sainthood out of it. "Tammi, you may not know my history here in Silvermine. I've been here a few years, since I got the job as library director, and I've been unexpectedly involved in sleuthing some murders. I have no intention of continuing that pattern. But of course, I can't help thinking about what happened last night, and I don't mind talking with you."

She went on. "I warn you, you might not like my conclusions. What if I decided that you were a diabolical mastermind? Whatever I come up with, what motivates me is finding out the truth, what really happened, not being nice to my neighbor or for that matter getting along with the policeman who happens to be married to the other librarian at work." Lauren recognized that she was putting her own twist on something that Hercule Poirot often said in the Agatha Christie mysteries.

Tammi sunk down into the recliner as Lauren talked, and Lauren thought that the expression on her face made her seem about eight years old. She had the look of a child yearning to be comforted. Combining that with her unmistakable sex appeal and tendency to wear her clothing rather tight, Tammi could get what she wanted in a lot of situations.

Lauren went into the kitchen and put the teapot on. Thinking that Tammi probably hadn't eaten, she pulled out the potato salad that she had made for lunch. She dished up two servings and took them into the living room, onto the coffee table. Tammi was staring straight ahead, her thoughts absorbing her.

"Here, have a bite to eat. Want some coffee or something?"

Tammi smiled politely, and again Lauren saw the appealing child in her. "Yes, thanks, black."

As they ate, Lauren said, "You know, I don't really know much about you or your life, even though we've been neighbors for a while. What was your day like yesterday?" She hoped her sympathetic tone would encourage Tammi to relax. At the same time, Lauren had an uneasy feeling that she had just opened a door that she would not be able to shut. But she meant to keep her promise to Justin that she would stay out of things that weren't her business.

Tammi's words came easily. Lauren hadn't been sure how talkative she'd be, but talking about the everyday details seemed to soothe her. "Well, I was glad that it was Friday, because it had been a lot of work all week over at the training facility. One of our staff members was on vacation and I was cleaning and walking dogs more than I usually do. I did get to train one of my favorite dogs, and that was fun. Mike wouldn't have liked how soft I am with her, but she's a sweet little dog and followed my hand signals nicely. Also, I like Fridays because I go bowling with Sam and Jane and some of the other women here in town.

So this Friday went like that, just getting some housework done and helping out at work. A friend of ours, a business associate of Mike's, came from Denver in the afternoon."

Lauren noticed some emotion from Tammi when she spoke of this person. She put that in the back of her mind and smiled to encourage Tammi to continue.

"His name is Tim Thompson, and he was Mike's boss at the chain pet store where Mike worked for a while. They got to be friends, and they talk business together a lot. He came here yesterday so the two of them could have a talk with spreadsheets and all that, about our business. Mike was trying to decide whether to take out a loan and open up a branch of his Dog Place in another town. Since it was a private discussion, they got together at our house instead of at the office, with both their laptops on the dining room table. I didn't pay much attention because business planning isn't my kind of thing."

"What is Tim like?"

Tammi looked at her hands as she answered. "He's real nice. He's older, you know, about fifty, and he listens to you. He's not handsome like Mike, but he has kind eyes. He's very smart about business, and he'll tell you straight out what he thinks. He was already kind of a mentor to Mike when Mike and I got together in Denver. He came to our wedding, which was nothing much, just a few people. His wife couldn't come because she had just had surgery... She died not long after."

Tammi paused, and Lauren asked, "Is Tim your friend as well as Mike's?"

Tammi looked out the window at the trees for a moment before she answered. "This is confidential, right? I wouldn't want people to know, but Tim has been wonderful to me. His wife was in the hospital in Denver a lot, she'd go in and out, you know, with complications. Well, it happened to be at the same time that my mom had cancer and was also in that hospital, over a year ago now. As much as I could get away from Silvermine without making Mike mad, I was spending time in Denver. Tim and I ran into each other a few times at the hospital, and we'd have lunch together. Or we had dinner at one of the little places near the hospital, and we'd just sit and talk. My mom is doing okay now, but I didn't tell Mike that so I could still get away to Denver sometimes."

Tammi stopped there, but Lauren had the feeling there might be still more to the story.

"So yesterday...?" Lauren asked gently.

Tammi stood up and looked out the window across the street at her house, as though it could tell her what happened inside its walls. "I think they had a good meeting. Mike was pretty cheerful, so I guessed that opening the new branch might be a go. I didn't hang around them much, partly because I hadn't told Mike about seeing Tim around the hospital and all. Mike can be, I mean could be, real possessive. So I felt a little awkward with the two of them yesterday, but when Mike invited Tim to stay for dinner, I just smiled and nodded. Tim left for a while, going over to the training facility to see how it was set up. He hadn't been in Silvermine for quite a while."

Mickey came back into the living room and jumped up on the sofa next to Lauren. Automatically, she fed him a couple of leftover bits of the potato salad. The soft murmur of Tammi's voice seemed to soothe him, and Lauren was glad he wasn't so afraid now. He dozed off on the sofa, his soft little head resting on Lauren's thigh.

Tammi glanced at Lauren as she sat back down. "As soon as Tim was out the door, Mike got mad at me for not being friendly enough to him. This is embarrassing... But probably your aunt next door heard us so I may as well tell you. Mike yelled at me and kinda shook me, and I screamed a couple times, to get him to stop shaking me. After that he did stop and he let me go grocery shopping."

Lauren thought to herself that you never know what's going on in other people's lives. "Thanks for telling me," she said, thinking that the police might not have heard this part of the story. She also wondered what Tammi might have left out of the telling now, too. Had those been the screams that had upset Mickey? It seemed likely.

Tammi played with her wedding ring as she said, "it feels really good to talk to you like a girlfriend, you know, somebody I can trust. You're being real nice. I thought with you being the head of the library and all, that you wouldn't be interested in talking to me since I'm not educated or anything."

Lauren laughed. "I'm the only one in my family to go to college. I grew up on the Front Range, in plenty of rough neighborhoods, since that's all my parents could afford usually."

"We have more in common than I knew," Tammi said. She yawned, and then she yawned again. "Talking with you is the first time I've relaxed all day. I think I'd better go check on the dogs and then see if I can't take a little nap."

Lauren smiled. "A good idea," she said. "Anytime, feel free to tell me more."

"If you really want to hear it," Tammi said diffidently. She left so quietly that Mickey barely noticed.

FIVE

It was only a couple of hours before Tammi phoned Lauren and asked if Lauren would like to hear the rest of her story.

"Sure, come on over. I'll be glad to talk for a while." Lauren had just cleaned the kitchen from lunch.

Once pleasantries were exchanged and Tammi was settled with a glass of iced tea, Lauren asked, "So what happened after you got back from grocery shopping yesterday?"

Tammi looked down at her wedding ring and twisted it with her fingers. She pulled a tissue out of her pocket and blew her nose, then wiped her eyes repeatedly. "Well, Tim came back to our place while I was out shopping, and he and Mike were deep into talking business again. I put together a quick meal and the business conversation continued through dinner. I was relieved because Mike was so caught up in that topic that he didn't really pay much attention to me. They were already back into spreadsheets on their laptops when I heard Sam's car outside, coming to pick me up for bowling. I had put on culottes to go bowling in, and I noticed that Tim saw where I had a bruise on my leg. I should have left my jeans on, I guess, to keep it covered. He gave me a questioning look, and I knew he would ask me some time how that happened. Anyway I left to go bowling."

"How did you get that bruise?"

"Oh, it was just one of those things that happens. Mike shoved me one day and I banged my leg on the corner of the coffee table. No big deal."

Lauren wasn't sure how far to push her questioning, but she figured she needed to know as much as she could. In as casual tone as she could muster, she asked "No big deal?"

Tammi glanced at Lauren but didn't quite meet her eyes. "Well, I guess a lot of men get a little rough sometimes. Mike did, but he loved me and he was always super sweet afterwards, so I never thought much about it. It wasn't anything, really. It only happened now and then."

Lauren said, "I wonder if Tim guessed anything." She was fishing to see what Tammi might say.

Tammi looked away. "Yeah, he would have. He saw another bruise I had, one time in Denver, and he asked me how I got it. I told him it was from Mike. That one was on my upper arm, after Mike shook me. Tim told me then that I didn't have to take anything like that. I was surprised, because I never thought it was a big deal. Anyway, when I left to go bowling, I hoped Tim wasn't going to say anything to Mike about the bruises, because I didn't want Mike guessing that Tim had become such a good friend to me, that he would stand up for me."

Lauren guessed that Tim and Tammi might be closer than Tammi had admitted. She put the thought on hold and asked Tammi what could have happened while she was away at bowling.

Tammi launched into a long-winded explanation of why she hadn't seen Mike on the floor when she first got home. "Well, I guess that Tim left pretty soon after that to drive back to Denver. Mike had had a couple of beers with dinner, but he wouldn't have been wasted by them. He might've gone over to the Dog Place to check on something or he might have done some more work on the spreadsheets. Maybe somebody else came by, I don't know. I guess they must have, because I think that probably Mike was attacked while I was at bowling. Then when I ran in to tell him I was going to have tea at your house, he would have already been lying on the kitchen floor. I wouldn't have seen him from the front door, if he was behind that island."

She went on, "It's just so hard to believe that he's dead. Why would someone want to do that? And what am I going to do?" She started crying hard.

Lauren wasn't sure what to say. Was Tammi such a fabulous actress that she could be faking this innocence? Had she killed her husband, who obviously was less than ideal? More likely, it seemed to Lauren, Tim could have brought up her bruises to Mike and they could've gotten into an argument. An argument that turned deadly. But from what Tammi said about Tim being so nice... well, she could be trying to protect him. Lauren remembered noticing when Tim left the house, whistling a happy tune.

"Does Tim drive a white car?" she asked.

"Yes. Why?"

"Oh, nothing really. But I noticed when he left. I don't remember the time or anything, I was reading. Tammi, you didn't notice anything that wasn't normal when you stopped in your house before you came over here for tea?"

Tammi's eyes moved as she tried to recall the scene. "You know the police asked me that too, and I told them everything seemed normal. But when I said that, something was tickling the back of my mind and I couldn't think what it was. I still can't, but let me think a minute... Oh, maybe things were a little messy in the kitchen, like the dinner dishes and maybe something else was different. Darn, it's hard to tell. Everything is different now and I just can't remember."

Lauren asked, "What about the pink leash?"

Tammi said, "There were always leashes around. I didn't pay any attention to leashes." She got up, saying that Lauren knew as much as she did about the rest of the evening. "My sister will be here soon. She's coming from Denver to stay with me."

She said a baby-talk goodbye to Mickey. He just looked at her, but at least he didn't bark.

Lauren felt drained after Tammi left. The death was such an emotional event, and she could feel herself getting sucked into the drama. Good thing that Sam was meeting her at the park soon, for a training session with Mickey. They would walk around, keeping Mickey on a loose leash as much as possible. They had done this once before, but Lauren wondered how Mickey would behave since he'd been so upset yesterday. That was only yesterday? So much had changed.

She took a leash off the hook by the front door, and Mickey jumped up, wagging his tail. She glanced up and down the street before opening the front door, but the only person she saw outside was Ryan, walking his Akita. They were a couple of blocks away, on the other side of the street, coming towards her, but Mickey was friendly with the dog and wouldn't bark at her. Ryan was one of the people she often saw out walking in the neighborhood. She knew him because he worked for the company that kept the library's computers running. He was in his late 20s and he and his girlfriend Malinda had a couple of kids. He was friendly enough, in a geeky sort of way.

She walked towards the park with Mickey, hurrying a bit to avoid Ryan. He could be very talkative.

The session with Sam went well. How could it be that Mickey was so perfectly behaved with her? They walked around the park, on and off the paths, first Sam demonstrating and then Lauren trying to do the same thing. The goal of the lesson was for Mickey to learn to walk on a loose leash.

"It's really quite subtle," Sam explained. "Not with all dogs, but Mickey is extremely tuned in to what you are doing all the time. That's both from his Sheltie and his Papillion ancestry, probably more from the Papillion, I'd guess, because Shelties as herding dogs tend to be independent thinkers. But for whatever reason, breed or just pure personality, Mickey focuses intently on you, even when you aren't aware of it."

Lauren looked fondly at the little dog, busily trotting along the path. "He doesn't seem to be paying all that much attention to me now," she said.

"Oh, but he is. Let your attention go into the leash now. Notice what happens when he gets to the end of the leash and starts pulling a bit. He's communicating with you in that moment. If you tug very lightly, that's a way that you can tell him that you don't want him to pull so much. Let's work with that for a few minutes here, and you'll see how quickly he gets it. I've noticed before how fast he learns. But if kids or other dogs come close, he's likely to pay more attention to them. Let's go down this little hillside where there aren't so many people."

Lauren was so used to walking Mickey with him pulling ahead on the lead that she doubted Sam's advice. Mickey was small, only about 25 pounds, so Lauren didn't pull hard on the leash herself. Usually when Mickey pulled hard, she just hurried up herself. But this time she tried giving a gentle tug, nothing that would hurt his neck, and within a few minutes, Mickey was walking on a loose leash. She noticed that when the leash became taut, he slowed up as if waiting for her.

"That's very cool," she said. "So I guess I need to practice that this week, huh?"

"You sure do," Sam said. "Soon we'll work on his barking, but first you are developing a method of communication with him by doing this with the leash. It will carry over into other means of communicating more closely. You could do this in your backyard, before you feed him. I've seen that he loves food as much as any dog alive, so practicing with him right before a meal is great."

They came to a bench near the river, and Sam suggested that they sit and chat there. "Mickey can play around you or get in your lap if he wants to, and his free time is a reward for a good session. Besides, I want to mention something to you."

As they sat, Sam glanced around and said, "I've been wondering what's going to happen to Mike and Tammi's dog training business. I can't imagine her keeping it going, can you?"

Lauren said, "I don't know if she has thought yet about what she'll be doing. She's got to be a major suspect in the killing. If she did kill him, she'll be doing time, I guess. But it seems to me that either that will happen or she'll leave and move back to the Denver area. She's got a sister there... the sister is here for a while."

Sam said, "I've got an idea..."

SIX

Sam looked at the river for a moment. Then she said, "Here is what I've been thinking about. When Mike came back to town and started up his business, I was really pissed. I was developing a good clientele for dog training and I was doing some boarding at my place, like I'm still doing. He undercut my prices, on purpose I'm pretty sure, though I have no proof. But my business fell off and it's been hard to make a living. But if that facility they've got turned out to be for sale, I've got some family members who might go in on the purchase with me. So if you hear anything, let me know."

Lauren watched Mickey curl up on the grass at her feet as she asked, "You didn't ever work there with Mike, did you?"

Sam said, "No. Mike had to have everything his way and I'm just too independent to work with that. And we have really different attitudes about working with dogs. He wanted to control them, and I'm all about observing what's going on in a dog's mind. Actually, we reflect two different schools of thought about dog training. He was old school, and I think he was clueless about the subtleties of dogs' minds.

"I'm into trainers like Ian Dunbar and Patricia McConnell and a bunch of others. I go to conferences with these people. I love trying to figure out what a dog is thinking, and it's such a rush when I get it right. Like seeing how Mickey is so attuned to you. He's just an amazing little being. I'm not sure you even know the half of it. Most people don't realize what's going on inside dogs' minds."

Lauren said, "I sure love him a lot, and I'm learning from Momo how to pick up what he's thinking, at least sometimes. We'll see if I don't know the half of it as we keep working on training. So I kind of get the feeling you are training the people as much as the dogs."

"Absolutely. By the way, I don't go where Momo can go in her mind. I've never been psychic. For me, working with dogs is about observation, watching body language mainly. But no criticism of her, she is a great woman. I'm one of many people who survived their teenage years in this town because we had her to turn to." Sam shifted her body on the bench. "And if there's any way I can get into that business, just keep your ears open for me okay?"

"Gladly," Lauren said. "Say, how do you think Mike died?"

Sam took a deep breath. "Have you ever seen any of the research on domestic violence?"

"What do you mean?"

"Well, it's obvious to me that Tammi was covering up some abuse from Mike. She's just the type to do that, so nicey-nice and sweet, such a darling little thing..." Sam's voice was sarcastic.

Lauren said, "One day at the library, I came across some violent death stats. About a quarter of murder victims were killed by family members and about half by someone else that they knew. I've been thinking about those numbers. They sure make the odds high that Mike was killed by someone who knew him. Of course, the pink leash makes that practically certain."

"Pink leash?"

"Yeah, didn't you see it?"

"It could have been right there, but I was so focused on doing CPR," Sam said. "But I've been thinking a lot about what happened. Didn't sleep well last night so I just lay there and thought. Seems to me that Mike could have been killed by a few different people. I don't mean more than one in the house, doing it together, though I suppose even that's possible. I think Tammi could have done the deed, sweet and darling as she seems. I'm sure Mike was roughing her up, when I think back on the times that we went bowling and she was sore in different places. Of course it could be that she's really accident prone, but I still think she's the main suspect."

"That's what the police seem to be thinking too, at least according to what Tammi told me earlier today. But it seems to me there are other suspects too, including you and me and Jane."

"Hey, back off!" Sam said.

"I don't mean that any of us did it. But there's an old saying about murder suspects, to look for motive, means, and opportunity, so at least in the abstract somebody could think of us."

Sam said, "Geez, let's hope they don't. Enough people know that I detested Mike's training methods that I suppose they could think that was motive for murder. That's ironic though, because my argument with him was always that he was willing to use physical force and I think it's counterproductive. This whole thing is spooky."

"Yeah, it sure is. I'm trying to stay out of being involved as a sleuth."

"Sleuth? You mean like you'd figure something out that the police couldn't?"

Lauren looked down. "It's happened before."

Sam nodded. She knew the stories of Lauren's involvement with what had happened one time in the library and another year out in the national forest. She looked around the park, seeming to make sure nobody was close enough to overhear them. "Well you're smarter than most people, that's for doggone sure. If it was my rear on the line, I'd want you on my team. Did Tammi ask you to help?"

Lauren felt herself getting in deeper. A little reluctantly, she said yes.

Sam whistled, a single long note. Mickey looked up from his nap, decided the whistle had nothing to do with him, and put his head back down on the lawn. "So how do you think Mike was killed?"

Lauren sighed. "Like you, I've been thinking a lot instead of sleeping. I do think it's possibly Tammi. But from the way she begged me to find out who did it, she'd have to be a very good actress. My favorite theory at the moment is a guy I don't think you know about. Tammi told me about him today. He used to work with Mike in Denver, and he was here in Silvermine yesterday. He was still at their house when Tammi left to go bowling, and then I saw him leave their place sometime later. I was deep in a novel, an old Agatha Christie one, and I just glanced up, so I didn't notice much about him. But he's the last person I know of to have been at their house."

Sam said, "Tammi mentioned him to Jane when we were bowling. I came back from the restroom and just heard the end of the conversation. It sounded like maybe she was hot for the guy."

Lauren said, "She's pretty close to him but I don't know if it's in that way. Anyway, I've been thinking that someone else could have gone into the house while you were bowling. Seems like there's always people in and out of there. I do keep wondering about the pink leash that was lying on top of Mike and then disappeared. Well, I've got a phone date with Justin this evening, and he's not going to be pleased when I tell him what's been going on."

Sam said, "Be sure to tell him how well Mickey did this afternoon. That's a great little dog you've got. And practice the leash connection a lot, starting as you walk home with him."

As Lauren had feared, when Justin phoned, he wasn't pleased. He was incredulous. "Seems like you are a magnet for the seamy side of life. Am I going to be safe, moving back in with you?"

"Justin! Of course..."

He chuckled. "Glad to know that. Say, it looks like I will be done with the work I'm doing here in a week or less. I'll need a few days at work in Fort Collins, to wrap things up there and to make arrangements for how I'm going to be a Forest Service consultant and work from Silvermine. So I'm guessing it will be about two weeks till I get home to you. Say, my brother Don might be able to help you understand what happened with Mike. He sure is connected with all kinds of people. Everyone needs their cars worked on. Don hears lots of news and gossip from his customers."

Lauren was relieved that Justin was giving her a tip. "I'm having dinner with him and Betty tomorrow, at their place. Your parents are still away on that little trip, and Momo's on her way to Mexico with Arnold, so it will just be the three of us. And little Rosie, of course, but she's way too young to understand the nuances of adult conversation."

"It won't be long until we'll need to talk in code," Justin said. "But honey..." His tone became tender. "Do be careful about sleuthing around. Don't hesitate to borrow Spunky from Don and Betty for the nights. There's something comforting about thinking of you having a Rottweiler in the house if I can't be there."

Lauren smiled. "There's no danger, Justin. I'm sure of that. All I'm doing is thinking. How risky can that be?"

SEVEN

LAUREN WALKED MICKEY the few blocks to Betty and Don's place for dinner on Sunday night. Over a delicious garden salad that Betty had made and chicken Don grilled outside, the three of them talked about what had been going on. Little Rosie was out playing with a friend in the neighborhood.

Of course, they knew about Mike's death. It had been on the news, and they had heard about it from a variety of people. "I called Momo on her cellphone," Betty said. "I told her about the death. She didn't have any ideas, and she said she hadn't given Silvermine a thought since they left. They are about to cross into Mexico from Texas."

"I didn't know Mike," Don said.

"You mean there's someone in this town you don't know?" Lauren teased.

"With over ten thousand people here, I'm sure there are a few," Don said with a laugh. "I was still a little kid when Mike went in the Navy, and it's just been a year or two since he came back and opened up Mike's Dog Place. Of course I've seen the building he uses, with that cartoon picture of him on the front. But that's not the same as knowing the guy. Yesterday I asked around to see what I could find out about him. You probably have heard most of this, but he played football in high school and hung out with the jocks. He smoked a little weed but mostly he stuck to beer. Sounds like he was a pretty straight kid, and actually it sounds like he stayed real mainstream. You know, wanting money and prestige. I don't think he sounds too interesting." Don laughed at his judgment.

Lauren outlined the suspects as she had thought of them, including herself in the list. "The only other person who crossed my mind was Ryan Campbell, for no good reason except that he does walk through the neighborhood a lot. I have no idea if he even knew Mike."

Betty served up baked apples with a dollop of ice cream. Don said, "I know Ryan. He was a year behind me in school. He's one of those geeks who's got a superior attitude, and I don't see much of him. I work on his Toyota pickup now and then... Right after high school... "

He stopped as the doorbell rang. It was a Rosie's playmate's mother, bringing Rosie home from her visit. "Welcome home, sweetheart," Don said. He picked the tired little girl up and gave her a big hug. "Want to come in for some dessert?" he asked the neighbor.

"No, thanks, Don, I've got to get my kids in bed," she said.

"Dessert!" Rosie said, but Betty had anticipated that and was already making her a small dish.

Lauren reminded Don that he had broken off a sentence. "What were you about to say about Ryan, Don?"

"Like I said, we rarely cross paths. Say, what makes you think Mike's wife didn't do him in? Often in domestic violence, the guy has been worse than anyone realized until the wife murders him in self-defense."

"At the moment I think it's more likely that it was this friend of theirs, a guy named Tim. He had been there for dinner and he was still there when Tammi went bowling. I got a glimpse of him, actually, though I didn't think anything of it, when he left their place and got in his car. At that point, he was whistling a cheerful tune, and I gotta say that doesn't fit with my idea of what a normal person would be doing after committing a murder."

"There are psychopaths out there," Don said. "Or he could be normal and trying to appear like nothing happened. But I'll stick with the wife theory for now."

Lauren said, "It would make sense to me for it to be this guy Tim if maybe he and Mike got into an argument, and I'm wondering if he might have brought up to Mike—as a friend—that Tammi had some bruises. In that case, since Mike had a couple of beers and was known to be possessive, who knows what might have happened?"

"Sounds feasible," Don agreed. "I'm curious who else you've thought of as possible suspects. "I know how thorough you are in thinking things through..."

She said, "Well, I suppose Sam is a candidate, especially since people know what a dim view she took of Mike. By the way, we had a great dog training session yesterday. Mickey is so tuned in when he wants to be. I'll show you what he can do soon."

Lauren shifted in her chair. "Maybe I could be considered a suspect too... I was home alone that evening. Momo and Arnold are probably clear because Mike was known to be alive for a few hours after they drove away, and it's pretty far-fetched to think they would sneak back. No motive there either. The only other person I know who was around there was Jane. Come to think of it, she did hate Mike because of the way he treated dogs, so there's motive, but I don't know if she would have had a chance. And to be complete with the list of everyone I saw Friday night, Ryan did walk by."

Lauren got a thoughtful look on her face. "I just remembered that after we went into Mike and Tammi's house, Jane didn't stick around. She suddenly said she had to leave. I didn't think anything of it at the time,... well, I guess I had a quick impression that she couldn't stomach seeing what appeared to be a dead body... but it never crossed my mind to think of it being anything more. I doubt it is, but if I'm going to be inspired by Hercule Poirot, I need to pay attention to everything."

Don got up from the table again, picked up Rosie, and started to carry her out for bedtime routines. For once, Rosie didn't complain. She looked plenty worn out from her play date. "Well, if I can help you with anything, just give me a call," he said.

Lauren smiled up at him. "Thanks Don, I really appreciate that. I'm looking forward to going to work in the morning and thinking about other things."

She and Betty lingered at the table. Betty said, "I know I inherited some psychic abilities from Grandma Momo, but I've never learned to just pull them up at will and I'm not sure I will ever want to. But I did try tuning in a little bit just now as we talked. Nothing came up, or just the same mishmash of thoughts that probably anyone would have."

Lauren took some dishes to the counter. Betty got up too, and together they quickly cleared the table. As Lauren prepared to leave, she called Mickey in from their backyard where he had been playing with Spunky. "Betty, I love you just the way you are, psychic or not. But what was your mishmash of thoughts? Maybe there is something useful in them."

Betty laughed. "You're incorrigible with your curiosity, Lauren. I promise you that if I have a single original thought about all this, I will tell you right away!"

Lauren accepted that. She didn't think Betty was hiding anything from her on purpose, but she did wonder what had gone through Betty's awareness. Still, Lauren went home feeling very satisfied about the loving connection with the couple who had truly become her family. Once Justin got back, she'd be encircled even more.

In the morning, she dressed with unusual care for work, choosing a deep brown long-sleeved T-shirt, a dressy one she'd gotten online with a pair of matching slacks. She wore her brown hair down, and put on a pair of cute sparkly green earrings that would show a bit through her hair. She added a patterned green and brown scarf to wear around her neck. For shoes, of course she always wore comfortable ones, given how much she was on her feet at work. Today it was a pair of brown loafers. She was amused that she was thinking so much about her clothing until she remembered that once before when she was involved in an untimely death, she was interviewed on television. She hoped that wasn't coming up again, but if it did, she'd look her best.

As was her habit, she left home to go to work about an hour early. Mickey had seemed nervous about being left alone, even though he normally was just fine. So she dropped him off for the day at Betty and Don's, as they had offered. The moment that Mickey saw Spunky, he ran off happily to play. Lauren was glad of the extra walking, over to their place and then over to the library. It was a lovely morning and the walking helped her get centered and calm. Funny how she always thought of herself as calm by nature, but she'd been plenty stressed over the weekend.

Walking through her neighborhood was so soothing. There were large trees everywhere, with wide trunks showing their age. Some of the old houses were a bit rundown, but most were in good shape. A few had been yuppified with fancy paint jobs and added on porches. Don and Betty lived in an area that looked like it had been built up in the 1950s or so, with a lot of brick houses. Don and Betty's house had a bomb shelter basement and a separate tiny apartment at ground level where Justin had been living when Lauren met him.

She turned her thoughts to the week at work. There would be a library board meeting tomorrow. She would have to present to the board her idea that it made more sense to add on to the present building—build an addition, move into the new part, remodel the old part, and be done with it—than to build a new building. She figured it would cost about half as much to get a really nice expansion job than to go for a totally new building. She knew that Margaret Snow, the chair of the library board, was very keen on the new building, but she was Momo's age and came from a more prosperous era. In fact, she and Momo were boomers who had gone to school together.

Margaret had worked in libraries for years until she had retired a few years back, but Lauren wondered if she was up to date on how library usage was changing. Now, a lot of libraries were using their meeting rooms as small business centers and for other needs in the community. Lauren thought it would cost the library district a lot less to keep up the comprehensive list of meeting spaces in Silvermine that Grace had compiled than to overbuild so they could be a venue for a variety of good causes. It happened that the town did have plenty of meeting space. Several churches were quite willing to have their halls used, for one thing. Also, City Hall had a room that groups used regularly.

It was going to take some courage to make her case to the library board. After all, they had hired her because she was the most enthusiastic of the applicants about a new building. She and Margaret had become very friendly since then, and she hated to disappoint her. Margaret was savvy about money, though, and Lauren hoped that she'd come around quickly. Whatever the plan turned out to be, they had to be allies going forward.

In the downstairs workroom of the old two-story library building, Lauren turned on the desktop computer and got the coffee machine going. Then she settled down to work uninterrupted. Usually Daniel Moore, the young janitor and shelver, would be cleaning, but it looked like he must have come in while the library was closed over the weekend. She had almost as much solitude when he was there as when he wasn't, as he was high functioning autistic and not chatty. A nice kid just out of high school, he had once helped her out a lot. She had learned from that how observant he was, without seeming to be noticing a thing.

Did she have the guts to push for what she thought was best? She knew that she could do the presentation, but what if she encountered a lot of opposition? Lauren thought of herself as professional and able to work things out with her board. She'd already had quite a lot of practice since coming to Silvermine, and she knew the board members generally respected her opinions. But this could be dicey, and she was aware that sometimes she gave in when she didn't want to. She could remember giving in many times, during her childhood anyway. But hey, she was a grown-up now and that should count for something. Was she lacking in the confidence she would need? She didn't think so. She certainly hoped not. She was amused to notice that wearing a slightly dressier outfit today helped with her confidence. She'd better dress well tomorrow too.

EIGHT

It was slow that morning in the library, and Lauren stayed downstairs in the office. She told the front desk clerk to buzz her if anyone needed help, and she did go upstairs when a man had a question about the timing of transplanting tomatoes. Thanks to Betty being such an expert gardener, Lauren had taken her advice and beefed up the collection of gardening books.

She was concentrating on her drawings of the remodel idea for the library board when Grace arrived a bit before noon for her shift.

"I came in a little early to catch up with you," Grace said. She looked at the papers Lauren had spread out and added, "that is, if you have some time now." Grace was wearing a beige summer dress that set off her dark skin. She too had a scarf around her neck, small multi-colored polka dots.

"Let's shut the door," Lauren replied. They still needed to keep their voices down if they weren't to be heard by people using the children's collection. She got right into updating Grace on everything that had happened from Friday night when Grace's husband Paul had been the responding officer, through the whole weekend.

"Paul couldn't believe it when you were there until you reminded him that you lived right there across the street," Grace said.

"I promised Justin that I wouldn't get involved, or rather that all I would do is think about it. And I've been doing that a lot," Lauren said. "I won't get in anybody's way. Paul teased me, or at least I think he was teasing. It's not obvious to me who did it or why."

Grace shrugged. "Growing up in D.C., I learned that the *why* of violence is often not clear. As for teasing, that's his way. He teases me a lot, and it's how he can tell me things that could be hard for him to say otherwise. He's always done that with the kids too."

Lauren had hoped that Grace would volunteer a bit more information about what the police thought but she was just sitting there. She would just have to ask right out. "Grace, without violating confidentiality, is there anything more you can tell me about the police investigation?"

"I knew you would ask me that, so I ran it past Paul. He said it's too early to know anything. The department will be working on the case this week. He asked me if Justin was back in Silvermine yet and I said not yet."

"I don't think I'm at any risk," Lauren said. "Mickey will certainly let me know if he thinks anything is amiss." She told Grace more about Mickey's trembling, barking, and running under the bed.

She didn't want to keep talking about the dangers, so she moved to the topic of the library plans. "Grace, what do you think about a new building compared to a remodel that would roughly double our space here? I'm sure the board will want to know your opinion as a librarian."

Grace let out a long breath, and Lauren thought that she was glad to be done talking about the death. "Well, I was pretty excited about the idea of a new library. But, we all know that the economy isn't as good as when they hired you. Here in Silvermine, people are a bit sheltered from what's going on around the country. With so many family members back east, and being members of a minority, Paul and I are more aware that many people in this country don't have enough food or decent places to live... and don't get me started on healthcare. Of course, anyone can know all this from the news, but I think he and I know it more viscerally. So a fancy new library doesn't seem quite as essential any more." She laughed. "Or does the board want it to be a daytime center for homeless people, like that famous branch of the San Francisco Public Library?"

"I expect we'll have some homeless people using the library, but you've been doing a great job with your story hours at the shelter and the other things we helped with last year have made a difference. I did design the public restrooms to be suitable for homeless use as well as ordinary use... I drew in two washbasins in each restroom, where we could have gotten by with one, so if a homeless person is washing up a bit, anyone else can still wash their hands. So you're saying that you are more in favor of the remodel idea?"

Grace nodded. "It will be interesting to see if the board agrees with you. That Margaret Snow is a pistol..."

"Don't remind me," Lauren said. "Really, I think she's the one to worry about. And I have been."

Grace said, "I'll pray tonight for the highest good, whatever that will turn out to be. Now I'd better get upstairs. I'm weeding the reference collection."

As Grace went upstairs, Lauren thought how glad she was to have her on the staff. She was the first person that Lauren had hired, and that was for a job on the circulation desk. Grace had become the head of the circulation desk and then Lauren had promoted her to librarian. Grace didn't have a degree in Library Science, but she loved helping patrons find what they wanted and she was savvy about using computers and the Internet. Lauren thought that Grace had picked up a lot of reference skills from raising four kids and helping them with their homework. And she was taking an online class in librarianship.

The workday passed smoothly, with nobody asking Lauren questions about her neighbor's death. There was no sign of any television crew either, to her relief. When she walked home after work, Lauren felt relaxed for the first time since Mike had died.

She grabbed a quick bite from leftovers, and walked over to Betty and Don's to pick up Mickey. He was glad to see her, and his calmness showed her that he'd probably been playing all day with Spunky and worn himself out. Nobody was home, so she just took Mickey from the backyard and mapped out in her mind a longer way home that would give them plenty of practice in loose leash walking.

At first, Mickey was pulling on the leash, so Lauren tried standing still every time he pulled forward. That was another trick Sam had showed her, saying that it was well known in positive dog training circles. For larger or more energetic dogs, you could also stop and then walk the other way but Lauren noticed that Mickey didn't need that much correction. He actually picked up on what she was doing within a minute or two. Most of the walk home was a delight for her. She had never known him to be so tuned in to her while on a leash. She went by a corner with a traffic light, and he heeled perfectly, waiting with her for the green light.

But when they saw a woman walking a dog about two blocks away, Mickey went ballistic. He almost succeeded in pulling the leash out of Lauren's hand. Lauren was startled but kept her hold on the leash, though she thought she had no control. As she and Mickey hurried down the sidewalk, the woman glanced back at them, smiled what Lauren assumed was a greeting, and lengthened her stride. Mickey didn't stop barking till the woman and dog were further away. Lauren wondered who they were. She thought she had seen the dog before but the woman wasn't familiar to her.

"Not your best performance," she said to Mickey. "I think we'll go out in the backyard for a bit of practice and you'll have to earn your food." He did, very well.

"I guess you can be a good little dog," she said. He responded by licking her legs.

She had a bite to eat and then the doorbell rang. Mickey glanced at her before running to bark at the front door. Lauren thought to herself that maybe that was what Sam had explained to her, how Mickey was forming a closer bond with her through the lessons and practice.

It was Tammi at the door, with a woman who looked so much like her that they could have been twins. On second glance, the other woman was older and had the wrinkled skin that habitual smokers end up with.

Lauren couldn't help saying the obvious. "This must be your sister, Tammi. Come on in. Would you like some iced tea?"

"That's real nice of you, yes, if it isn't much trouble," Tammi said. "Yes, this is my older sister, Marty. We won't stay too long."

"No problem, the tea is already made up and I don't have anything I have to do."

They settled down in the living room, Mickey in Lauren's lap where he could keep an eye on the sisters. Tammi said that she was sleeping better with her sister around and that she was beginning to think about what to do next.

"There will be a memorial service for Mike later. We're still working on the details, but it will be at the Baptist Church. There is a woman there who is a fabulous singer, and she is a client of ours. She boards her little Yorkie with us when she travels, and that's quite a lot, as she sings all over the country. I'm waiting to set a date for the service until she comes back from the tour she's on. I do hope you'll be able to come, Lauren."

"Thank you. But tell me, how are you feeling, Tammi?"

Tammi's eyes were red from crying and she hadn't bothered with makeup. "It really got to me that he's gone. The finality keeps hitting me in the face. Marty here has been trying to get me to think about my life and the Dog Place and all that, but I'm lucky to be able to think five minutes ahead."

Marty hadn't said a word yet, but she made up for it now. "Tammi honey, you know I want the best for you, and I just think it's best for you to get out of this little town." She turned and smiled at Lauren. "We aren't used to small town living. We're city girls through and through. So I say Tammi needs to get back to Denver, back with her girlfriends and regular life like she had before she fell for Mike."

Lauren hadn't expected this tidbit of sisterly advice and it surprised her. "What about the police, Tammi?"

Before Tammi could say a word, Marty went on. "Tammi can give them my address and phone number and those of our other relatives. She's not running away from anything. Besides, it's absolutely ridiculous to think that she would have been the cause of Mike's death. Thank God he didn't kill her, you know he wasn't always nice."

Tammi put her hand on her sister's arm.

"Oh, you mean the people around here weren't clued in to what a sleazebag you married? I thought it was obvious from the get-go that his charm was fake and that you got bruises from him."

Lauren thought this was one sister who didn't mince words. She wondered if Marty wasn't hard to take for Tammi right now, but at least she had someone familiar to help her get through the days.

NINE

Lauren stretched out in the recliner and decided to visualize the presentation to the library board that she'd be giving in the morning. She had deliberately left her laptop at the library, as she didn't want to obsess about the details of her talk. Of course, she wanted to create a good feeling at the meeting. She knew that both Margaret Snow and the fundraiser Karen Smith would be surprised and displeased at her suggestion for the remodel. They would think she had lost her vision. Well, maybe she had, but realism had a place in this world.

Here she was focusing on the reaction she didn't want. Better to think about what she did want. She decided to move forward in time in her imagination, and she spontaneously found herself picturing that she and Margaret and Karen were having lunch at the cute little French restaurant where they had met once before. She imagined that the lunch was about a week from now, after the board meeting.

Lauren had read books about how visualization creates energy that then manifests in physical reality. She had had enough experiences herself in doing this to know that sometimes it worked. She didn't have it figured out why it worked sometimes and not other times. Maybe it had to do with her subconscious thoughts, just as she had been thinking a moment ago about Margaret and Karen as her adversaries. But she didn't buy into the approach that everyone created everything in their lives. She thought that if she could visualize a satisfying meeting in her mind with Margaret and Karen now, it would be interesting to see how things unfolded in reality.

She pulled her afghan around her in the recliner, as the evening air coming in the windows was cooling. Mickey jumped up on her lap and snuggled into a comfortable position. She stroked him for a moment and then took a couple of deep breaths. With philosophy, afghan, and dog all in place, she was ready to go into the restaurant scene.

She imagined meeting Margaret and Karen at the restaurant. She clearly saw how they sat down and ordered lunch. They chatted for a few minutes, laughing and joking.

"Now that we've had time to think about your presentation, Lauren, I can see that you made a lot of really good points," Karen said. "I think you took everyone aback because the entire context for years had been a new building."

Margaret nodded. "I still think that if board members and the Friends of the Library worked hard, we could get a the votes for a new library. But when you placed the concept of a new library in the context of all the needs of the community in these times, I followed you. I think the City Council would be so relieved that they would be solidly behind the remodel. A smaller bond issue—combined with a pretty good-sized mill levy so the library has the funds for ongoing operation—has a great chance of passing as soon as this fall."

As they ate, the conversation stayed light. The Lauren who was visualizing all this in her recliner noticed that she could fast-forward easily while still keeping the sense of reality that was so absorbing.

Karen proposed a change in the design, to have ramps instead of stairs between the floors, with a small coffee bar with a few tables. The present children's area could be part staff work space and part meeting rooms for small business or other uses. They would end up with even more space than a new building might provide, with plenty for computer labs and the new airy children's section. It had always bothered her how the children's section on the lower level was so dark.

"Great," Lauren said. "I'm thinking we have a winner here." The three women held up their half empty coffee cups, clanked them together, and laughed as they finished their coffees.

Lauren felt relief wash through her body, both in the restaurant as she visualized the meeting and in her body in the reclining chair. She really liked these ideas. Well, no wonder, they were things she had been thinking about! Visualization was interesting, how it drew on her existing ideas and embellished them.

In her recliner, Lauren smiled. She felt Mickey's sleeping body in her lap and the afghan wrapped around her shoulders. She stretched, opened her eyes, and got up. As she tidied up her house a little before bed, she suddenly realized that for over an hour she had given no thought at all to what had happened across the street. What a relief.

She slept like a baby, and the next morning the board meeting was almost anticlimactic. She mentioned all the details that had come up in the visualization. Nobody liked her concept of remodeling instead of getting a new building, not even with the coffee bar and ramps. What she hadn't expected was that it didn't bother her in the slightest. She was calm and cheerful as she answered all their objections. They agreed to give her proposal some time.

TEN

LAUREN WENT HOME for lunch, pleased with the meeting. She had left Mickey at home alone for the first time since his big scare, and she wanted to be sure that he was doing okay. He greeted her as usual, and she relaxed at the kitchen table, eating leftovers and reading a magazine. Suddenly Mickey started barking, and he ran into the living room and barked from the recliner, his usual spot. Lauren suddenly remembered that she hadn't locked the front door after her when she came in.

An older man in business clothes, someone she didn't know, was at the door. If he was a salesman, she'd get rid of him in a jiffy. Oh, wasn't he the guy she had seen leaving Mike and Tammi's house the night of the death?

If so, what was he doing here in the middle of the day? Tammi had said that he worked in Denver at his corporate job. She went to the door, put her hand on the knob, and paused. Justin's brother Don, an expert in security, had once warned her not to open the door to someone unless she was sure of them. He wouldn't be pleased that she'd left the door unlocked either.

Well, this man was one of the suspects. Lauren went to the window next to the door and called out, "Hello." Mickey growled, deep in his throat, but he was quiet enough that she could hear over him.

"Oh, I'm so glad you're here," he said with a friendly smile. "Tammi must still be out... she and I had a date to meet here. I've just arrived from Denver, and I'm wondering if you'd mind if I used your bathroom while I wait for her. Tammi told me about you, or I wouldn't have bothered you."

Again she almost opened the door. Again she paused. "No, I'm sorry, I'm on my lunch hour and have to go back to work. Besides, my boyfriend would be furious if I let men we didn't know into our house when he's not home. But you can go down to the library three blocks from here and use that restroom, or go on downtown and there are several."

If Tim could have been the killer—and he seemed to her to be one of the more likely suspects—he could also kill her. Lauren wasn't going to take risks. That wasn't strictly true about Justin, but close enough.

He gave her a little wave through the window and dashed across the street. Lauren noticed he checked carefully for any dogs in Tammi's back yard before opening the gate. He disappeared behind the house, and idly she wondered why. Maybe he really did need to pee.

Lauren immediately locked the front door and brought her lunch into the living room where she could keep an eye on any doings at Tammi's house. Mickey watched her eagerly. She picked up a bit of ground beef and walked across the room. She didn't have to call him... He was right at her feet. She asked him to sit and gave him the piece when he did.

As she ate her lunch, Lauren thought about the encounter with Tim. At least he didn't try the front door. What would she have done if he had? He seemed very polite, but then some serial killers were said to be charming. She shivered.

Tim was certainly a contender as a suspect. She knew that murders were often completely unplanned. She considered the theory that Tim might have confronted Mike about Tammi's bruises and they could have had an argument. Mike was certainly the stronger of the two of them, but Lauren was pretty sure that Tammi had said that Mike had drunk a couple of beers. Well, that could mean more than two beers, the way people spoke. So maybe Mike swung at Tim and in self-defense, Tim hit him over the head with something, a frying pan or whatever.

"Think more about the personality of Mike," Hercule Poirot said in her head.

Lauren wasn't expecting a conversation with the famous fictional detective who was featured in so many of Agatha Christie's books. "I beg your pardon?"

Poirot said, "It's very simple. To figure out any murder, you must think about the victim. You must think of every little detail, especially the ones that nobody else will consider. Always, always, these little things matter very much."

Lauren wondered where the voice was coming from. Was she cracking under the strain? Glancing at the clock, she decided she had time to listen to the voice a bit more before going back to work. Then she closed her eyes, to find out if Monsieur Poirot had any more to tell her.

She let details of the crime wash over her. As she did, she realized that she had been thinking about people other than Mike.

"You see?" Poirot said. "I have explained it perfectly in several of the books I'm in. You must know exactly the kind of person the victim was. That will tell you so much. My dear librarian, you too must think this way."

What was Mike like? She had hardly known him, but she'd had a gut level dislike for the way he spoke to her. Mike manipulated with his good looks. She had felt that he was being condescending in pouring on the charm, often with a little smirk.

She'd heard others say that he needed to be right. There was a ruthlessness to him. Sam didn't think he cared all that much for dogs, beyond seeing them as a way to be successful in business. Success did seem to matter to him, and so did money.

What sort of person was Mike? Who was he at heart? Lauren felt a chill run through her as she realized that Mike made her feel that she wanted to be anywhere else other than with him. She wouldn't go so far as to call him evil... But Mike was always all about Mike. His success, his wife, his charm. So he was wrapped up in himself, and it seemed to her that he could justify any actions of his in the context that it worked for him. That made her feel creepy. She'd known few people who were so completely absorbed in their own desires. Odd that she hadn't realized it before.

But thinking back to what Hercule Poirot had said, how was thinking about Mike going to help now? Well... Mike would be disliked by a lot of people, maybe most people, whether they realized it or not. So what? Most people didn't go around murdering people they disliked. So was this really getting her any further down the road? She felt more confused than anything. She would let it all percolate and go back to work.

She left Mickey dozing on the sofa and hurried back to the library. She practically jogged along the streets, the charm of the old houses lost on her as she thought about Mike, Tim, and the sudden appearance of the Belgian detective. With all that, and the visualization she'd done about the meeting with Margaret and Karen, her imagination was certainly getting a workout.

Grace wanted to hear details from the board meeting.

Lauren shrugged. "There really isn't much to say. I explained what I had in mind, and nobody liked it. They all had pictures in their minds of a new building, and a remodel seemed tacky to them. But really, Grace, the odd thing is that it didn't bother me one whit."

Grace nodded. "You did what you felt was right. How things will turn out remains to be seen, but you did the next step. Good for you... Not everybody could go up against that board."

"It wasn't so hard. I guess I was clear enough that I just did it. Well, an afternoon of routine work sounds like the ticket for me. I think I'll work on the book order for fiction. I've gone through most of the shelves, and I'll do the mysteries now. You know, one of the problems with keeping up the fiction collection is that people eat chocolate while reading novels. It's obvious from the stains on pages!"

"The other thing I've noticed about fiction is that it disappears," Grace said. "I think we lose more of the how-to nonfiction, though."

"When I was in library school, we had some discussions about that," Lauren said. "It's amazing how many people seem to think that not returning library books is okay. People don't think of it as theft evidently. No wonder a lot of libraries use pretty drastic measures with patrons, cutting off their privileges if they're late and so forth."

Grace said, "Speaking of crimes, I've been thinking about Mike's way with dogs. We boarded our German Shepherd with him once, and Paul refused to ever do it again after he picked her up. He told me they hadn't treated her right."

" I was just thinking that a lot of people must have disliked Mike."

"No doubt about that," Grace agreed.

Lauren immersed herself in going through the old mystery books. She ended up with a pile to discard, a pile that needed mending or new covers, and a few notes for some classics, such as Agatha Christie's books, to replace. Mostly they would beef up the collection with newer titles. It was satisfying to get the simple task completed.

Sam and Jane were coming over to her house after work for dinner. At least, she didn't have to cook much. They would be bringing pizza. Sam knew that Lauren was allergic to wheat, and she had promised that one pizza would have a gluten-free crust. Lauren got home in time to take Mickey for a short walk, hoping he would be better behaved around Sam after some exercise. She had plenty of garden greens that Betty had dropped off, and she whipped up a huge salad.

ELEVEN

THE WEATHER WAS MILD, and they ate in the backyard. Jane had brought a couple of her little rescue dogs with her, and Mickey played happily with them. Jane always had one or two rescues at her house, along with two preschoolers, her husband, and their own dogs.

Lauren wondered aloud how Jane managed it all.

"It's pretty easy most of the time," Jane said. "I don't have a job, so I can do all this. Billy works for the hospital... they hired him for bookkeeping but when they found out what a Mr. Fixit he is, they added maintenance work. It's not fabulous pay and the schedule varies, but I also get some money from my ex, enough that I can stay home until the kids are in school."

Lauren thought to herself that Jane's passion for dogs overrode any more ordinary concerns like new clothes or nice housing. She and Billy had bought a ramshackle little house with a big yard in a poorer part of town. Billy worked on it sometimes. Jane seemed to enjoy her own kids by treating them like puppies. She never seemed to worry about her kids and the dogs that passed through their place, but then she had taught them from very early on how to be around dogs.

Lauren had heard her say to her son one day in the park, "Be a tree!" The little boy had frozen in place, his arms wrapped around his body. He was enjoying it, even when a large barking dog ran up to them. Jane had explained that being a tree was a widely used method, taught to kids everywhere, that had greatly decreased the number of dog attacks kids suffered.

Lauren brought the conversation around to Mike, watching Jane closely as she did so.

"Excuse my French," Jane snorted. "There are no polite terms in English for that guy. The world is a better place without him."

Jane had never had any use for Mike, but that was a strong statement.

Lauren asked, "Who do you think killed him, Jane?" She noticed that Sam was watching Jane closely as well. Might Sam be on the same page with her, wanting to see if there was any chance that Jane had been the killer? But the two of them were such close friends that Lauren doubted Sam would go there.

"Doggone if I know, but they did the dogs of this town a real favor." Jane crossed her arms, while a cold smile played across her face. Lauren wondered if Jane's obsession with dogs made her indifferent to the sanctity of human life. But then she realized that she herself thought Jane was correct. Probably the dogs of Silvermine would be better off without Mike's presence. Especially if Sam managed to get the facility and run it in the way she would, with much more love and respect toward the dogs than Mike had been capable of. Of course, what Tammi would do with the Dog Place was still unknown.

Lauren said, "I keep wondering about that pink leather leash that was on top of Mike when we ran over there. I thought at the time that it had been wrapped around his neck, but it wasn't there when they took him in the ambulance. Maybe it was just lying on top of him and it fell to the floor when they picked him up. What do you two think?"

Jane said, "I was so freaked out when we went in there and Mike was dead that I hardly noticed anything."

"But why did you know he was dead? I couldn't tell," Lauren said.

Jane said, "He looked dead. That's all I can say. So I don't remember any leash of any color, the main thing was my feeling of having to get out of there." She looked down and added, "Sorry I left it all for you to to deal with... I didn't even think about that."

Lauren had thought that Jane belonged on the list of suspects, but now she was less sure. She'd have to think more about Jane later. She wondered what Sam thought and looked over at her.

Sam had put her hand on Jane's shoulder and was patting it gruffly. " Did you think then Mike had a heart attack?"

Jane said, "it wasn't that exactly... I just thought of death. With that blood on Mike's forehead, I suppose somebody could have killed him ."

Lauren said, "Jane, how did you get home that night?"

Jane squinted as she looked at Lauren. Raising her voice, she asked, "Why do you ask?"

Lauren wondered if she had hit pay dirt with that question. She diffused the tension by smiling, leaning forward to touch the back of Jane's hand for a moment, and saying in a soft tone, "Well, I just wondered about it, since you'd had a ride over to this neighborhood with Sam and she didn't leave here till later."

Jane let a breath out and said, "I was going to phone Billy to come get me, but I knew the kids would be in bed by then and I didn't want him to leave them. When I walked out the front door of Tammi's house, I didn't know what to do, I was just so upset. But then I remembered that Tammi had a bicycle in her backyard that I had seen when I was over there one time. So I took it and rode home. I brought it back on Saturday."

Sam swatted at her arms. "It's getting to be bug season, have you noticed? I think you have both mosquitoes and black flies here in your yard, Lauren."

"Let's go make some tea in the kitchen and sit in the living room," Lauren suggested.

Dusk was turning to dark as they sat down with their mugs. Sam glanced across the street and said, "Doesn't look like anybody's home over there."

That reminded Lauren of the odd request she'd had at lunch time from the older man from Denver. The three of them chewed that over for a while, and Lauren wondered aloud if he hadn't committed the murder.

The conversation lightened up when Jane described her latest successful rescue placement. "This one was the sweetest pit bull I've ever met. We had her at our place last week, after she was discovered out by the highway. The guy who found her knew that the shelter was overloaded with bully breeds and that she wouldn't have much of a chance of being adopted from there. He works with Billy, so he'd heard that I was a sucker for rescuing dogs... they had talked about it on their lunch hours. Anyway, he brought the dog over the evening that he found her. She was way too thin and had obviously been on her own for a while. I just fell in love with her right away. She was so gentle and loving that I named her Sweetie Pie on the spot. I fed her by hand at first that evening, since she would have eaten too fast."

Jane went on, "We put her out in that little kennel we have in the back yard, and she slept through the night without a fuss. In the morning, the kids were thrilled and she was great with them. I could tell that I'd want to keep her forever if we kept her very long, and Billy insists that we've got more than enough dogs, so I got on the phone and made a bunch of calls. We found her a home with some good people that next day. I took her to the vet, and the people picked up the bill and had her spayed right away. She's doing great with them, I hear."

Sam said, "Always love to hear a happy dog story. She's a good dog. I went over to Jane's and checked her out. She knew sit, down, come, roll over, and a few other things. If Jane had kept her longer, I would have done a session or two, to make her even more adoptable. Say, isn't that one of the college kids who works at Mike's training center over there knocking on Tammi's door?"

All three of them could see the young man and hear the knocking. It escalated to pounding. "I know that kid," Sam said. "He's the brother of one of my clients. I'll go see what's up." She was halfway out the door by the time she finished her sentence.

Lauren and Jane could tell that when Sam joined him, the young guy was gesticulating wildly and talking loudly, though they couldn't make out what he was saying. He had arrived on his bicycle and almost immediately he left the same way.

TWELVE

SAM CAME BACK to Lauren's living room. "If it isn't the darndest thing," she said. "What's his name there was riding his bike to work at Mike's Dog Place a little while ago, and as he got a few blocks from it, he came upon one of the dogs that was being boarded there. It was loose and running down the middle of Main Street. The kid, I think his name is Ben, pulled over and called the dog who came right to him. Ben had some rope with him so he fashioned a leash and rode along with the dog beside him. But almost immediately he saw another loose dog from the place, this one on the other side of the road. Fortunately it was after rush hour. So he and dog number one went over to dog number two, who was glad to see them. Ben had another piece of rope and pretty soon he and the dogs were traveling along together again. But danged if another loose dog from the place didn't turn up. Ben was out of rope, so he just whistled and that one followed them.

"By the time he got down to the center, he had six boarded dogs that were coming along with him. Thank God, none of them were hit by cars. He's on the evening shift by himself, so it took some doing to get all the dogs back in their pens. They had been in the outdoor kennels, and someone had unlocked the back gate and unlatched each of their doors. Ben was pretty freaked out when he couldn't reach Tammi by phone. He wasn't sure if he should call the police to check for fingerprints or what. So he decided to close up tight – the padlock for the back gate had just been thrown in the bushes, with the key in it, weird huh? So he locked up, put the key in his pocket and rode over here."

"I wonder where Tammi's got to," Lauren said. "And what about her sister? And what about that friend from Denver?"

"No idea, but I told Ben that I would go down there and give him a hand on my way home. I think it would be good to call the police, since this could have some relationship to Mike's death, but I'll do that once I'm there. Jane, how about we take off now and I'll drop you at your place? Thanks for a nice evening Lauren. I'll take the leftover pizza that's on a wheat crust, okay?"

"Please do," Lauren said. "And give me a call when you have any news. I'll be up for at least another hour, and I can run down if you want any help."

"Okay, but I don't think we'll need you," Sam said. "Come on, Jane, let's make tracks..."

Lauren puttered around, cleaning up the kitchen, letting Mickey out into the backyard for his final pit stop, and brushing her teeth. It took her a while to relax, and she stayed in her jeans as she surfed the Internet a little bit. When her phone rang, she was right on it. It wouldn't be Justin this late, since he was back east, two hours ahead of her.

"Can you get down here fast?" Sam asked. "It's too unbelievable to tell you over the phone. Wear old clothes so you can help us clean up."

"Sure, be right there." As she checked the doors and promised Mickey she'd be back soon, Lauren thought that her intuition had worked for once. She had completely expected this call. Strange.

She drove across town to the Dog Place. Nothing looked amiss other than the single police patrol car parked in front. Lauren parked behind it and hurried into the building. Normally things would be locked up tight this late, but the front door was open. Inside, she saw Sam with the young guy who worked there and Paul Johnson. There were five or six dogs in the indoor kennels, two dozing and the others watching the people.

"Did you figure out anything more about the dogs getting loose?" Lauren asked them.

"Nope, didn't give that a thought," Sam said. "We were too busy getting an ambulance for Tammi. At least, I thought it was Tammi when Ben and I went in the building and saw her lying here on on the cement floor, but when the EMTs moved her to carry her out to the ambulance, I was surprised that it was her sister. I haven't met the woman, but she looked so darn much like Tammi that I knew that's who it was. Don't worry, she'll be okay, but she had a nasty blow to her head and I expect she's got a concussion."

Lauren couldn't breathe for a moment as her stomach tightened up. Tears came and she blinked. She looked again at the three of them. After this news, they looked different. She saw the tension in each face. She remembered that Paul had once commented that you never get used to death, and she could see it in his face now, especially in his eyes and in the tightness around his mouth. She had a sudden flash of empathy for the emotional price that he paid to work in law enforcement.

"Where is Tammi, at the hospital with her sister? How did it happen?"

Sam said, "Good questions. Tammi was seen leaving town earlier this evening, as a passenger in a white car driven by an older man."

Paul questioned Sam and Lauren whether anything had been going on at Tammi and Mike's house, and Lauren told him about her encounter with the man wanting to use her bathroom. Otherwise, the house had been quiet during the time she was home. Paul made a few notes and said he'd be on his way.

Lauren said she would go over to the hospital and at least tell Marty hello.

Sam asked Paul, "Okay if we clean the blood up off the floor? Otherwise, the dogs will be licking it like crazy when we let them out."

"Yes, I got some photos, and I've got a blood sample here." He held up a small plastic container. He added, "Lauren, I'm going to stop by the hospital now too. I'll see you there."

She nodded and glanced at the other two. Sam and the boy both looked drained. "I'll come back by here as soon as I can," Lauren said. "Do you think you'll still be here?"

The boy said, "I have to take care of the dogs."

Sam said, "Yeah, if you aren't gone long, Lauren. If you get back here and the lights are out, call me on my cell phone. Come on, Ben, I'll give you a hand. Let's start with the blood on the floor."

The hospital wasn't far. Nothing in Silvermine was far, Lauren thought, as she pulled into the emergency room parking lot. She met up with Paul in the lobby. It had been a quiet night and Tammi's sister had already been seen in the emergency room. She was being moved to a room, to be kept overnight for observation. Paul said to the receptionist, "We'd like to speak to her for a moment."

The receptionist said with the flat voice of someone who had seen too much, "Room 112."

As they went in the room, Lauren remembered Tammi's sister's first name. "She goes by Marty, I don't know her last name," she said to Paul.

Marty was awake and conscious, but far less talkative than when Lauren had met her before. "Hey, Marty, I came by for just a minute. How are you doing?" Lauren said.

"My head hurts like crazy and I'm dizzy," Marty said. "What happened?"

Lauren smiled. "That's what I wanted to ask you. What do you remember?"

"Tammi and I stopped by Mike's training place after dinner. I had my car and that friend of theirs named Tim was going to follow us back to Denver. We all had a nice dinner at a steakhouse out on the edge of town. I remember all that fine. I don't remember much after that. Oh, we were about to leave the Dog Place and I went to use the restroom. Something hit me hard... and later I heard sirens. And now I'm here. Where's Tammi?"

Lauren heard Paul's little intake of breath. She said, "I don't know, Marty. I'll try to get a hold of her as soon as I can. Try to sleep and I'll come by in the morning. I don't work till noon tomorrow."

As she prepared to leave, Paul said to Marty, "I'd like to ask you a few more questions...This is serious and we'll want to get ahold of your sister right away." Lauren left before the conversation went any further.

THIRTEEN

Lauren tried to sleep, but her mind was racing. Whoever had killed Mike could easily be the person who had attacked Tammi's sister as well. She guessed that the person thought the sister was actually Tammi. Leaving the hospital, she had driven by the Dog Place, but it was dark. She had talked briefly with Sam by phone, but that had yielded no new information. Sam said she thought that it could have been a vandal who had let the dogs loose for distraction before looking around to rob the place.

Lauren wondered if there could have been cash or veterinary meds there that someone would break in for. She wished she could sleep, and she thought of getting up and walking around to discharge some nervous energy. But she just lay there groggily, thinking and thinking. Before she finally dozed off, she had a thought that seemed fruitful, and she promised herself she would follow up on it in the morning.

She slept in a little, as she wasn't due at the library till noon. She didn't remember her late-night insight until she was eating breakfast. What was it, something about Jane? What she remembered didn't seem significant. She took Mickey for a walk around the park, paying close attention to the leash between them. He was very good. She left him at Betty and Don's so he could be with Spunky. Then she got dressed for work and went over to the hospital, where Marty was in bed.

"I will be discharged," Marty said. "But no way am I going to drive to Denver today. I guess I'll go back to Tammi's house and stay in the guest room. It's a little creepy there, but not too bad."

"I'll be at work this evening," Lauren said. "I can check up on you when I get home, though. Where's your car?"

"Car? Geez, I lost my smarts. It's over by the Dog Place, in their parking lot."

Lauren thought that maybe Marty shouldn't be driving yet. "Well, I expect it's safe there. Why don't you take a taxi over to Tammi's? I need to get to work, or I'd take you. Do tell me if you remember anything more about how you hit your head..."

"I didn't do anything, somebody whacked me."

Lauren had already guessed that. "Somebody whacked you on the head?"

"Yes, I think so, but what I remember and what I might be imagining are mixed up. Do I have any scrapes on my left elbow or knee?" Marty displayed the left side of her body, removing the sheet over her, and indeed her elbow and knee were neatly bandaged.

"Well, it looks like what I remember is true. Somebody hit me on the head, and I kind of remember falling down and the person beginning to drag me a little ways. Then I heard a man's voice say "shit," and he took off, I guess. I don't remember more till I heard the siren really loud. Maybe I was in the ambulance by then."

Lauren said, "I'll stop by the police station on my way to work and tell them this bit."

"I don't have much use for cops, but maybe your small-town ones are more honest. Tell them whatever you want."

Paul was at the station, working at a computer. Lauren told him what Marty had told her, and he said, "Yes, that fits with what she told me last night."

Lauren went on to work. Some days, it was a pleasure to just focus in on work. This would be one of those days, she thought, if she was able to pull it off. Before Grace left for lunch, Lauren filled her in on what had been going on.

"I'm just going home for lunch and I'll be the only one there. That makes it a fine time for me to get some good praying in. That's about all I can do," Grace said.

"Thanks, I appreciate that."

Lauren helped a couple of people find books, and showed someone how to use Google for basic research. She was about to settle down with the book order she'd been working on, when Ryan Campbell came in, carrying a briefcase. He strode to the row of computers and unscrewed the case from the one at the left end.

She went over to say hello to him. He was such a geek... He had walked right past her without noticing her.

"Hey, Ryan," she said. "How's it going? The computer that we had trouble with last week is the third one over. It was incredibly sluggish, to the point that we just put an 'Out of Order' sign on it."

Ryan glanced at her and said, "Hey yourself, that old computer is always slow. You should dump it. But I'll see what's going on with it while I'm here. I'll go through all your computers for a quick look, since I don't get here that often. Hey, there's been a lot going on in the neighborhood, hasn't there?"

Lauren nodded. "Too much, if you ask me. I hope things quiet down before Justin comes back for good."

"Oh, where is he?"

"He's been working in Fort Collins for over a year, coming home some weekends, and he's just finishing up an assignment in D.C. I'm not sure how long it will be till he's back for good. He's going to become a consultant for the Forest Service, or maybe work part time for them. But that will give him a chance to begin something he's dreamt about, doing permaculture out on his folks' land, you know, on the edge of town. Actually he and I are buying half that land—that'll be 20 acres—from his folks. Say, I don't remember you wearing sunglasses in the library before. Are you going incognito?"

Ryan's smile looked more like a grimace. "Not a chance in this town... You ought to know that by now. No, actually, the light hurts my eyes sometimes, and I've been having a spell of that. But tell ol' Justin hello for me when you talk to him. Sounds like all of the Russells are big into gardening. Did you know I've known Betty since we were kids? Heck, I even had a crush on her in middle school. I hope she doesn't remember that. More to the point, I hope my girlfriend doesn't remember it. Say, didn't Justin build a greenhouse on the back of your house? Are you growing much in it?"

Lauren thought to herself that you could talk gardening with practically anyone in town. She wouldn't have expected Ryan to have much interest, but evidently he did. "I've got some veggie starts I need to transplant into the backyard and some nice hanging planters with flowers and herbs, but really right now its most useful function is the little potty area for my dog. I can't always get home when I expect..."

"Tell me about it," he interjected. "What with viruses and malware, the computer business is booming. I'm glad I make a good rate for overtime, because I've had so much of it. Malinda isn't thrilled that the kids are usually in bed before I get home."

"I'll take that as my cue, and get back to work myself," Lauren said.

"Before you go off, there's something I'd like to ask you," Ryan said, lowering his voice. He glanced at the chair next to him and Lauren took him to mean that he wanted a more private conversation than they'd been having while she stood there. She sat down next to him.

He nodded and spoke softly. "I've been wondering how things are going at Mike's Dog Place without him there. Is Tammi doing okay? Mike could always handle my Akita but I don't think she can."

Lauren wondered why this part of the conversation needed to be private. "I doubt she knows yet what she's going to do. It's true that she's much softer with dogs than Mike was, but that's not necessarily a bad thing. For example, think of Sam's approach to dog training. I'm taking some lessons from her right now to help me with my little Mickey, and she's very gentle."

Ryan said, "Yeah, Sam has a natural authority that dogs respect. We used her for some training for the Akita before I got to know Mike." He quickly glanced around and lowered his voice further as he said, "I was wondering if they needed any help over there. I could find a little time to give them a hand if necessary."

Lauren thought to herself that once again small town neighborliness popped up from unexpected sources. After all, Ryan had just been saying how busy he was. "I think they probably could use some help, because Mike did a lot of the work there and so did Tammi. As far as I know, she's out of town now. Last night Sam helped out when they had a problem. You could call the place and I'm sure someone could tell you if they need anything."

"Thanks, I will," Ryan said. "Have you heard anything about a memorial service for Mike?"

"Tammi told me the other day that it would be at the Baptist Church because there's a woman there with a wonderful singing voice, but it's been postponed till that woman is back in town."

With his hands already deep into the guts of the computer in front of him, Ryan's nod was both recognition of what she'd said and dismissal. Lauren was happy enough to get back to work herself. She had that book order to finish up.

FOURTEEN

When Lauren walked home from work after the late shift, it was a lovely evening with still a little light in the sky. She had worked through her dinner hour, just eating some leftovers she'd brought to work. Don brought Mickey over from their place a little later and she told him that she had been chatting with Ryan.

"Did he tell you that he had a crush on Betty in school?" Don asked. "I swear, he must still have a little bit of the crush, because he's mentioned it to me more than once. His girlfriend is nice looking, so I was tempted to make up a story about noticing her in school, but I'm a couple years older than them and I don't remember her at all."

"Yes, he told me about the crush. He also quietly offered to help out at the Dog Place if they need it."

Don nodded. "Seems like he's settled down to being a good citizen, after being pretty wild for a while there. Don't think I ever told you about him after high school. Well, I'd better save that for another time and get on home. Bring Mickey by any time. Rosie had a great time playing with him in the yard."

Lauren had settled down with her email before she remembered that she had told Tammi's sister that she would touch base with her this evening. With a sigh, she got up to go across the street. Mickey was snoring gently on the sofa and scarcely noticed when she went out.

Marty was watching television and looked livelier. "I think I'll go back to Denver tomorrow and see if I can't find that sister of mine. She's not at my place, or at least she hasn't answered the phone there. I wonder if she ran off with that guy."

Lauren asked, "Do you think she would? She's had so much on her mind."

Marty snorted. "I don't know... she could be staying with one of her old friends around Denver. The sooner she's out of here for good, the easier it will be for her to get on with her life, if you ask me. I'm ten years older than her and I've always watched out for her. Not that there was anything I could do while she was under Mike's thumb. Hey, come look at this... I think I found the murder weapon."

Marty walked into the kitchen and opened the door of the little chest freezer. Sitting on top of other things was a frozen leg of lamb. Even from a little distance, Lauren could see that there was blood on it, along with a few hairs. "Holy Cow," she said, reaching toward it.

"No, no, no touchee," Marty warned. "That sucker could have fingerprints on it."

Lauren said, "I'd better tell Paul."

Marty let out her breath. "Well now, do we really have to tell the good officer about this? They seem to be so fixated on my little sister as the villain and chances are—since it's her kitchen—that her fingerprints would be on the leg of lamb."

Lauren sighed. "There's a famous short story about a woman who murders her husband with a frozen leg of lamb and then she cooks it and serves the lamb to the police officers who come to investigate. It's by Roald Dahl, who's better known for that kid's book, *Charlie and the Chocolate Factory*."

"Never heard of any of that. I don't read much. But hey, that's a good idea. Maybe I'll cook it up right now," Marty said.

Lauren said, "Not such a good idea, because we both know about it now. I sure don't want to keep information from Paul. I'd better just tell him, and after all, it could exonerate Tammi if someone else's fingerprints are on it."

Marty reluctantly agreed to leave it alone. She also agreed to leave her keys to Tammi's house on a nail under the back porch, in case Lauren needed to get into the house.

It had been a long day, Lauren thought, as she went back home. She called Paul at home and gave him a quick update about the leg of lamb. Before she could get that nice hot shower, her phone began ringing. She grabbed the cordless phone and flopped down on the sofa next to Mickey.

"Hey, it's Sam. Sorry to call you this late but I wanted to touch base with you about what's going on at the Dog Place. Do you have a few minutes?"

"Sure," Lauren said, with just a quick tinge of regret. "What's been going on there?"

Lauren could hear Sam letting a big breath out. "Well, quite a bit. Last night, after you and Paul went to the hospital, I helped Ben clean up the blood on the floor. It had soaked in and was difficult to get out. We probably should have let a big dog loose to lick it up. But seriously, I had time to chat with Ben as we worked. He's a great kid, and he told me a few things that he shouldn't have, maybe because he knows me from training his sister's Golden Retriever. He's been at her place a couple of times when I've worked with the dog."

Lauren suddenly felt more awake. "How long are you going to keep me in suspense?"

Sam chuckled. "I'm not going to. Ben has worked for Mike since the place opened, and he knew Mike pretty well. He said that Mike was sometimes really hyperactive. Ben is just out of high school, taking a few courses at the community college, and I could tell he was hesitating about saying something. I assured him that I had been around the block a few times and that nothing he would say could shock me. But still, I was startled when he said that Mike's occasional crazy hyperactivity reminded him of people using meth."

Lauren was dismayed. "Meth... I would never have thought of that, but then how often do I think of meth users? Rarely since I left the Front Range and moved to this idyllic town."

Sam let out a cynical laugh. "Idyllic! I like your idealism. Sure, I grew up here, I've seen a bit of the rest of the world, and there's no place I'd rather live. But girlfriend, this is not heaven. There has been plenty of meth around here, so when Ben said that, my mind started clicking on who could have been involved. Mike must have been circumspect about using it and that's not typical of the users I've known. But it makes sense to me that Mike could have been using it as a kind of super work enhancer."

Lauren felt a pain in her gut. She tried to breathe into it and noticed that she had tensed her whole body. She relaxed her shoulders consciously, but her attention was more on Sam's news. "How does this affect who might have killed Mike?"

"It opens it up. That guy from Denver is far from the only suspect, that is, there are no doubt more people who could have done it, people somehow involved with meth and the money around it. You know, everyone thought that Mike's business was doing well financially, and he gave off that vibe, but you know I've got a dark and suspicious mind. Now I wonder if he was running a meth business on the side."

Lauren said, "I've never been around meth, Sam. If you don't mind my asking, have you?"

"Yeah, I tried it twice, seven or eight years ago. I knew a group of people who were into it here in Silvermine... but it scared the heck out of me. I could see myself going down that road and I could see that the ending wasn't pretty. Some of my friends were already messed up. I went back to just booze. But it's not easy to leave meth alone if you like it. I probably was tempted to try it again dozens of times before I got to where I could leave the desire behind me. So that makes me really think about Mike. If he did sell it, how much did he use it? And does it tie in to his death?"

"Darned if I know," Lauren said. "I'm practically in shock. Well, it's getting late, but there won't be any sleep for me anytime soon, I'm sure."

"I've got more to tell you. This part is about dogs. Ben told me that he's worked the evening shift there since it opened. He says that a lot of times they only had two or three dogs overnight. Geez, that's no more than I often have in my place.

He also told me that when his sister needed help training her Golden, she asked him if he could get her a discount rate at Mike's, since he worked there. He told his sister not to use Mike, because he thought Mike was not a good trainer for soft dogs like hers. He suggested that she call me, and he told her he'd like to be present to see my methods. It turns out that this kid is pretty darn interested in dogs himself. He's even fantasized about becoming a veterinarian if he could afford the schooling."

Lauren said, "I bet you know where my mind is going. I'm picturing you running that place, with Ben one of your employees."

"I'd love it, nothing better. But before we hang up, I want to run past you another raving of my suspicious mind."

"Sure," Lauren said. How much crazier could things get?

"I wonder if somehow Jane could have killed Mike that night."

FIFTEEN

Lauren noticed her stomach doing another flip-flop. "Well, you know the old saying about motive, means, and opportunity. For Jane, the motive part is the easiest..."

"Yeah, she hated Mike's guts. You know what a soft heart she has for any dog, and what a hard heart she can have toward any person who mistreats a dog..."

"Marty told me what the means could have been," Lauren said, wondering if it would be okay to tell Sam. She had a sense that maybe she shouldn't, and she regretted what she'd said. But Sam didn't pick up on it. Why not? Maybe Sam knew things she was keeping from her too, Lauren thought.

Sam said, "Cool. But about Jane... You wouldn't know she had any opportunity that night, but I don't think I mentioned to you that when we got to the bowling alley, my pager went off. One of my clients was having an emergency with her dog freaking out, and I left Jane and Tammi at the bowling alley for about an hour. I went and took care of that, and then I went back and joined them. I didn't keep this from you deliberately, but it didn't seem that important at the time. But it does mean that I don't know what Jane was doing during that time."

Lauren said, "I thought you and Jane were such good friends..."

"Yeah, we're friends, but I still have to wonder if she could have done it. I've seen her get insanely furious at Mike. She cares a heck of a lot more about dogs than about people."

Lauren let it percolate and changed the subject. "Say, are things running okay at the Dog Place? I mean, will they just shut it down? Who would make the decision to do that? Tammi's out of town. Evidently she left last night. Besides, there must be some dogs being boarded there—maybe some of those that ran loose last night—whose owners are on vacation and don't even know what happened to Mike."

Sam said, "Ben and the other employees are keeping it running for now. If you manage to get ahold of Tammi, please give her my phone number and tell her I'd like to run it, at least temporarily. Say, we had some help this evening from Ryan Campbell, you know him, don't you?"

"Sure, I know him. He does the tech work on the library computers and he was in today. He asked me if he could help out and I told him to call over there. By the way, he said that you had a natural authority with dogs, and he mentioned that you had worked with his dog before he started using Mike."

"Yeah, that's nice to hear. I've known him since school. I remember he had a big crush on Betty for a while... he practically stalked her. Anyway, he came by for a couple of hours and helped do some chores. He's a hard worker, gotta give him that. He said the company he works for took care of Mike's computer and that it needed a little anti-virus work, so he did that too."

"Do you think he could be a suspect in Mike's killing?" Lauren had wondered about him from time to time, but she could think of no motives.

Sam paused a moment to think about it. "I'd sure rather it be him than Jane, but that doesn't make it so. He has his reasons to be careful, what with his well-paying job and all. Off the cuff, I doubt that it was him, but who knows? By the way, he'll be away for a few days, he told me. He and Malinda had a little vacation already planned with the kids, and they are going off in the morning. He asked me if I thought he should change that to help out, and I said no. Say, those kids are real cute. Malinda and both the kids came by to pick him up. They even look a little bit like him, though one was a toddler and the other one a baby when she and Ryan got together."

"Oh, I thought they were his kids," Lauren said. "I will never catch up with all you natives in knowing who's who."

"You're not missing much. You can remember this situation because it's just the same as Jane and her husband, that the kids are from Jane's first marriage."

"I'd forgotten that one," Lauren said. She yawned. "Well I better get to bed and see if I can sleep. I've got to be at the library early tomorrow."

Sleep was fitful, but she dragged herself to work an hour early as usual. The quiet morning time was precious for keeping on top of her work load. She exchanged a few words with Daniel, who had already cleaned downstairs. She didn't really notice him as he worked upstairs.

Lauren jumped a little when a tap came on the downstairs back door. People rarely came to that door. She left the workroom and went through the children's area. Ryan was standing at the door, with a small bag in his hand.

He said, "Sorry to bother you so early, but I'm about to take off with Malinda and the kids, and I wanted to install a computer part before we go."

Lauren wondered if he knew that she came in early or if he just took a chance on being able to get in. "Daniel Moore is working upstairs, so better call to him if he's doing the bathrooms, so you don't startle him," she said as she let Ryan in and locked the door again. "And please leave this way when you're done."

"Will do," he said.

It wasn't very long before he was ready to go. "Sam tells me you were a help there yesterday," she said as she let him out.

"Glad to be of service," he said with a little bow.

It was a satisfying work day, a nice balance of tasks at the computer and helping library patrons find what they needed. Margaret Snow phoned in the afternoon, to report that she and Karen Smith had just had lunch at the French restaurant and that they had both come around to being in favor of the remodel that Lauren had suggested at the board meeting. "I think it will be an easier sell to the city fathers, and Karen has some more ideas for the remodel itself," she reported.

"Great! You didn't even need me there," she said.

"No, we wanted to speak frankly and we didn't know that we had both come around to your idea until we were well into the conversation. Does that bother you?"

"Not at all," Lauren said, thinking that Margaret would be quite surprised to know that Lauren had been in on the conversation in her imagination. Margaret suggested they schedule a board meeting to discuss what to do next.

After work, Lauren got in a good stint of gardening in the back yard. Justin called and they caught up with each other on everything. He didn't remember Ryan from school, being several years older than Ryan and Sam, and Lauren was relieved not to hear again about the crush Ryan had had on Betty.

"I can't wait to settle down with you, honey," Justin said. "It's been a long stint working away. But I think it will be worth it. I've got a good amount of savings to put into the permaculture projects out on the land. Have you thought any more about whether you want to build a house out there early on?"

"I don't want to, Justin. There is so much that we'll be doing with plants, and plants take time to get established. If we choose a space for where a house could go sometime, then I think we're good. Hey, we could get a cheap old trailer to keep out there, as a place to take a break. We could even attach it to the water system when we get that in."

"Sounds good," he said. "I was thinking of putting a crude outdoor shower up someplace, but being able to shower inside—away from bugs—and change clothes sounds good. Hmm, changing clothes makes me think of something else we could do after cleaning up. Let's put a decent bed in there..."

"Justin, chill! I don't want to think about you without clothes on, not till you get here!"

"It could be a little sooner than I told you," he said. "I'm flying back to Colorado tomorrow and then I'll be in Fort Collins briefly."

"Great! It can't be too soon for me," she said.

"I'd like to think you're referring to my magnificent physique, but is that murder getting you down?" he asked.

"Yeah, some," she admitted. "It's a complex situation. But thinking is all I'm doing, like I promised you. Oh, excuse me, another call is coming in, and it's one I'd better take. Love ya, Justin!"

"You too, take care," he said.

The other call was from Tammi's sister Marty.

"How was your trip back to the Front Range?" Lauren asked politely.

"It was okay but never mind that. I can't find Tammi! Nobody has seen her." Marty's voice rose.

Lauren thought that not all women in their thirties told their big sisters everything about their lives.

Marty went on, her voice louder and faster. "Not one of Tammi's and my friends knew she was back in town. You know how you thought Tim might have murdered Mike? What if he killed Tammi?" Her voice broke and she was wailing into the phone.

Lauren didn't know what to say. She couldn't honestly reassure Marty that it was impossible. She just managed to say, "There are other suspects too, now. But nobody knows... except the one who did it." She wished she could be more comforting, and she thought she'd call the local police right away and say that Tammi might be missing.

SIXTEEN

Lauren woke up feeling awful. She was hot and her body felt like it weighed a ton. She managed to turn over, and Mickey crawled up from where he had been sleeping at her feet. He licked her hand where it was sticking out from under the covers, and that woke her up a bit more. At least she wasn't stuffed up... she didn't feel like she had a cold. She opened her eyes but took none of her usual pleasure in the pretty bedroom or the art on its walls.

Slowly she got up, let Mickey out into the backyard, took a shower, dressed in her sweats, had a cup of coffee, and began to feel slightly more human. Why was she feeling so drained? It could be all the stress of the week walloping her.

Her mind wandered back to the sick days she used to take as a child. Funny how often they occurred right after she had been to the library and had a new stack of books. Her mother must have noticed that correlation, but with a large family, she had been easy-going about what Lauren did, especially since Lauren always had the best grades of the six kids. Well, nowadays Lauren rarely missed work, but she thought maybe her body was telling her something today. Like enough already!

What did she have to do at work today? It was Friday, wasn't it? Wait a minute, she had worked last Friday, so Grace would be working today and Lauren would be working tomorrow. That was the regular schedule unless they traded if one of them had something special to do. There weren't any trades lined up. She must be really out of it not to remember that today was a day off.

She didn't feel up to her usual walk with Mickey, so she went out in the backyard and tossed the ball for him for a little while. Then, after a bite to eat, she stretched out in the recliner. She had her Kindle right there and thought she would read a while, but she began to reflect.

A week ago this evening, Mike had been killed in his kitchen. That was after she had come home to find Mickey trembling under the bed and she had seen Momo and Arnold off for Mexico. On Saturday the shock had left its mark on the whole day, and Tammi had asked her for help in figuring out who could have done it. Then Lauren had had a dog training session with Sam at the park, and Sam had confided that she was hoping to take over Mike's Dog Place. Nothing special had happened on Sunday that she could think of, just dinner with Betty and Don. On Monday, after work, Tammi had brought her sister over to meet Lauren, and later Lauren had had that cool visualization of having lunch with the chair of the library board and the fundraiser.

Continuing through the week, on Tuesday after the board meeting, she'd been home for lunch when Tammi and Mike's friend—the guy Lauren still thought could have been the murderer—had asked to use her bathroom. She had said no. She'd had a spontaneous vision of a conversation with Hercule Poirot, in which he had advised her to focus on the victim. That evening, someone let loose the dogs in the outside pens of the Dog Place, and Tammi's sister was hit on the head at the facility and taken to the hospital. She and Paul Johnson had talked with Marty there.

The next day at work, Ryan had offered his help at the Dog Place, and that evening Marty had shown her the frozen leg of lamb with blood on it. Lauren had called Paul about the leg of lamb. Then Lauren had talked with Sam, who had the idea that Mike could have been dealing meth. After that shock, Sam had gone on to say that Jane could be a suspect in the murder. Sam's imagination rivaled her own, Lauren thought.

At least yesterday was okay. She'd had a good talk with Margaret about the library and also an encouraging talk with Justin in the evening. Then Marty called, panicked that she couldn't find Tammi and worried that Tim could have killed her.

Not your normal week, thank goodness.

Lauren let the memories wash through her mind. She hoped that they would somehow arrange themselves in a way that made more ense, but they didn't. She figured that there were at least four suspects. She just didn't know enough to make any kind of educated guess about what had happened. Not that she cared for Mike's sake, but she just couldn't leave the puzzle alone.

She felt a moment of intense loneliness, even though Mickey had climbed up into her lap at some point when she wasn't noticing. She stroked his soft fur and he snuggled happily. But Lauren wished that Justin was home, or at least that Momo wasn't away. Sure, there were other people who cared about her, like Don and Betty, or Grace at the library. And all three of them had been very helpful during the week. Lauren realized, not for the first time, how much of a loner she was in dealing with her own emotions.

She really should open up more to her good friends. Heck, Don and Betty were even family. Maybe she'd invite herself over there for a meal and talk more with them about how stressed she was. Or she could invite them over here if she had the energy. Whatever.

She asked herself if fear was tapping her strength. There had certainly been scary moments, but she didn't think anyone was out to get her. Why would they be? She had had very little to do with Mike and Tammi as neighbors. If somebody thought she knew how the murder had occurred, that would be different. Then she'd be scared out of her gourd. There had been very frightening moments other years, after that library board member had been found dead in the stacks and later around the time of those two other deaths. What was it with her and murder? Why did she get so involved in sleuthing? That would be one for a psychologist, and maybe she should think about getting some therapy. She would talk that over with Justin sometime.

She reached for the phone and called Betty and Don. They agreed to come over for an early dinner, bringing a salad from Betty's garden. She would grill something in the backyard... That was easy. She could manage that, no matter how drained she felt. Now, what was she going to do? Groceries, laundry, housework, watering Momo's plants. Oh, and training Mickey some. She had an appointment with Sam for Sunday afternoon. At least, she didn't have to think about his exercise today. Spunky, his Rottweiler friend, would come over with Don and Betty.

She was about to drag herself into doing chores when a little movie came into her mind. Still on the recliner with Mickey in her lap, she closed her eyes and let the scene play out. She watched as her imagination showed a figure hurriedly going to Mike and Tammi's house after dark, getting into an argument with Mike, Mike threatening her, and the woman picking up the leg of lamb that was thawing on the kitchen counter. She saw Mike slap the woman's face and she saw the woman defend herself with the frozen meat. The woman was Jane. Lauren watched this interior movie, as tense as if she were watching an old Hitchcock masterpiece. She saw Jane burst into tears, throw a leash down, and hurry out.

What should she make of that? Was it just her imagination going wild again, or might it be something to take seriously? She just couldn't tell. Maybe later she'd have more insight.

Halfheartedly, she got up and put a load of laundry in. She was able to get her chores done, bit by bit. She even did some gardening. It was a beautiful day, she noticed, but to her everything felt flat. She took a nap in the afternoon, and that helped a little. When Betty, Don, Rosie, and Spunky arrived, she was grateful for their company.

She had meat and veggies on the grill and soon they were sitting outside, eating dinner and only having to swat the occasional mosquito. Missing Justin as she did, it was easy for

Lauren to notice how much Don resembled his older brother. They were both tall and lean. Don had black hair and blue eyes where Justin's were brown and brown. Don usually had a more serious, intense vibe than Justin, and tonight was no exception.

"So, Lauren, are you still obsessing about Mike?" he asked.

Lauren bristled. "Not about Mike. I really can't say that I've thought about him much at all, other than to hope that Sam can take over his training business. But how he died, yes, I guess you could say I'm still obsessing about who would have done it."

Betty said, "That seems natural to me. Heck, I've thought about it a lot too. I've tried to tune in psychically for anything that might come up, but when my mind is rattled my deeper intuition just isn't there."

"I can sure understand that, Betty," Lauren said. "When my mind is rattled, I can hardly even think."

Don leaned forward. "Lauren, I don't get it why you have a dog in this fight, if you'll pardon the expression."

SEVENTEEN

Lauren had to laugh at the way Don put it. "I was wondering this morning if maybe I should go see a psychologist some time. But for now, being my own psychologist, I think my dog is why I have a dog in the fight. I was so upset last weekend when I got home and Mickey was cowering under the bed. I think that's the main reason why I have a personal stake in this mess. But who wouldn't care if a murder happened across the street from them?"

Don stretched his long legs out under the table and leaned back. He looked at Betty, and she picked up the thread.

"Don and I are concerned for you, Lauren, that you're letting this get to you," she said. "Isn't there anything we can do to help? Justin called Don the other day, and they talked about it..."

Don's restless movement clued Betty. "Oh, wasn't I supposed to tell her that? Well, duh, we all love you and we are all family. So let me go back to my question. How can we help?"

Lauren's eyes filled with tears. She looked at the two of them, now side by side in the swinging love seat. "You guys are the greatest. If there's anything you can help with, I'll tell you... Oh, what if I were to tell you the story of my week, start to finish, and see if you can pick up anything I've missed? It's all such a jumble."

Betty and Don both agreed. Lauren went through it all, much as she had done by herself in the morning, adding in background details that they might not know. As she went along, they commented on one little bit or another, filling in things that Lauren hadn't known about the various people. She'd never heard about Sam being a suicidal teenager, but

Betty remembered. That must be what Sam referred to when she had commented that Momo had helped her get through her youth.

Still, the overall picture of the murder was all nuances and details. Don summed it up, "There is too much that is unknown. Did anyone else go into that house? Who could have wanted Mike dead? Or, like you mentioned, Lauren, was it Tammi or Jane or even someone else acting in self-defense after Mike got mad at them? Maybe I'll ask around among my customers." He chuckled, but Lauren knew he meant it.

Lauren felt a lot better after they left. Nothing like being cared about.

In the middle of the night, Lauren was jolted awake by Mickey barking beside her ear. He was standing on the bed, leaning into her right shoulder, and his body was rigid as he barked. Groggily, Lauren listened for sounds. Hearing nothing, she got up and listened at the back door, the front door, and windows on either side of the house. She still heard nothing. She peered out the shades next to the front door, but saw nothing. When a noise had awakened her in the night a few years ago, a man had actually been there and she had called the police. But she couldn't call the police just to report that her yappy little dog was barking. She certainly didn't want to be a laughingstock at the police station, if she wasn't one already with her obsession with sleuthing.

Mickey stopped barking while she was checking. When she got back in bed, he curled up by her shoulders rather than in his usual spot by her feet. He was trembling again. She patted him, massaged him, and talked softly to him. It soothed him and actually she felt better too. Rather to her surprise, she fell asleep quickly.

In the morning, she decided not to leave Mickey home alone while she went to work. Lauren thought that being with Spunky all day would be better.

Once at the library, she worked on the dog books. Sam had given her a list of books that she thought the library should have and she had offered to donate a couple if they didn't already have them. "Get rid of the really old books," she had advised. "Or at least, make a pile for me to take a quick look at." Betty had done something similar with the gardening books when Lauren first arrived in Silvermine... that was part of how they had become friends. The gardening collection was much larger than the dog section. She figured that she could get through the dog books before lunch.

Weeding books was aptly named, and it brought the same satisfaction as weeding in a garden. Things always looked better and there was more space afterwards. If books on the shelf looked ratty or old, people were much less likely to touch them. Lauren forced herself to handle even the most unappealing books, in case they were worth keeping, maybe with a new cover on them, or if they had information that she should replace with newer titles. Nobody had ever weeded the library collection much before she came. She had gone through the cooking, sewing, and other 600s when she first moved to Silvermine, but she had only weeded lightly in the pet section back then. Today she was determined.

By the time she stopped for a break, she had a big pile of books to discard, a small pile to ask Sam about, and some notes. It was evident by flipping through any given book what approach it took to dog training. Some of them were completely old school in admonishing the reader that you had to be the boss... if it said you had to be dominant, it reminded her of older books on raising children.

Sam had explained to her that newer methods of dog training were more attentive to how dogs thought. The library had nothing by Dr. Ian Dunbar, a veterinarian turned dog trainer, who was one of the leaders in this field. Sam had told her that one insight she had picked up from him was that dogs learned in ways that were location-based. In other words, if you taught your dog to sit or to roll over, or whatever, but you only practiced this in your kitchen, the dog would be much better at following your cue in the kitchen than anywhere else. So you needed to practice anything in a variety of locations.

The library was slow enough that she got all the pet books weeded, and Lauren had a peaceful evening at home with Mickey. She expected she would sleep well again, as her everyday life was being restored. Tomorrow she had a date to train Mickey in the park with Sam, and she would learn if there was any news. She figured someone would have phoned her if there had been anything significant.

Lauren slept well at first, but once again Mickey woke her up in the middle of the night. The nights were pretty warm in late June, and normally there were several windows that she left open. But she hadn't this time... She had gone around the house and made sure that doors and windows were all secure. It just seemed like a reasonable precaution. Don had once installed some window latches for her, a few years ago when someone had tried to get in. The latches provided a little air at the bottoms of several windows, so the house cooled off during the night.

This time, Lauren woke when Mickey started trembling. He had crawled up next to her again, and she woke to feel him shaking. A low growl was rumbling in his throat. Not expecting anything, Lauren still rolled out of bed to take a look around.

Her heart beat faster when she looked in the living room and saw the silhouette of a person—it had to be a man from the shape—outside the front window. Forcing herself to move closer to the shadow, without making a sound, she got up to the front door and flipped on the front porch light. That got rid of the man in a hurry. She almost had to laugh at the speed with which he left, jumping over most of the steps to her porch and taking off down the street.

But this was real. It was serious. She looked at the clock. It was nearly 3 AM and a man was trying to break into her house. She picked up Mickey and held him in her arms as she stood thinking. This could have been Mike's murderer. She grabbed her phone and punched in 911. Mickey was trembling, and so was she.

EIGHTEEN

She scarcely had time to put on a bathrobe and to put Mickey out of the way in the greenhouse before a police car pulled up in front of her house. Two officers came up the steps. Lauren recognized the woman... She had come to the library, how many years ago was that? Three? She'd never forget the morning that a dead body had been discovered in the nonfiction stacks.

"I remember you," Lauren said, waving the woman into her living room. "You came to the library that time..."

"Yes, I remember that too. What happened just now?"

Lauren described what had happened just then and the night before. She also mentioned the death across the street.

The woman said, "Paul filled me in on that yesterday afternoon. Good timing, huh? I doubt this person will be back tonight. We'll just take a look around outside and inside, if that's okay with you."

Lauren nodded. Both the police officers looked around with flashlights before telling her to call back if she needed to.

Lauren let Mickey back in and made herself a hot milk. She sat down with it at the kitchen table. She had stopped trembling, but she could feel her body's tension. She thought of herself as generally unworried about the fears that so many women lived with. Maybe because she was tall and fit, but more likely because of the way her father had taught her. "Men are sometimes not so nice to women, honey," he had told her when she was only about eight or nine.

She hadn't liked what he went on to tell her, but he had drilled her quite a few times on what to do if various scenarios came about. If a man she didn't know asked her on the phone if she was the only one home, if a man wanted to come into the house, if a man stared at her intently when she was riding public transportation, if a man touched her anywhere on her body without her permission, if a woman did any of these things... She had learned her lessons well, and now she thought they had been good for her. She was the oldest of the kids, and the ones right after her were boys. She didn't know if he had taught the boys or her younger sister later in the same way.

Did she have more courage because of all that? Really, those times had been like little visualizations that gave her some skill when situations arose. She remembered the incident that took place when she was in high school. It was rare for her to be home alone at night, but on that winter evening the rest of the family had gone in their old station wagon across town to a championship basketball game that one of her brothers was playing in. She liked basketball, but she had gotten permission from her mother to stay home and work on a big history term paper. She was concentrating on it, her books and papers spread out all over the sofa, when their next-door neighbor in the apartment complex knocked on their door. He was a middle-aged single man whom she didn't like much.

She automatically remembered her training. She thought of not even answering him, but one front window shade was partly up and he had probably seen her studying in the living room. She called out as if one of her brothers was in another room, and then she told the man that if he wanted something, he should come back the next day. He said okay and left. She was proud of herself for the way she had handled that. But, she remembered now, she had been on edge until everyone else got home.

Well, she was certainly on edge now. She hoped the officer was correct that the would-be intruder wouldn't be back tonight. She would borrow Spunky from Betty and Don from tomorrow night on. No longer the puppy he had been when she first met him, Spunky was a magnificent large dog, a Rottweiler, devoted to his family and protective if needed. Mickey had done his best these two nights — and Lauren realized she was quite sure now that someone had been at the house both nights — but there was only so much a small dog could do to intimidate. Yes, with Spunky in the house she would be safer. She briefly considered going over to Betty and Don's house to sleep but saw no reason for it.

The hot milk and her thoughts combined, and she could feel herself relaxing. She settled down to sleep, Mickey curled up next to her. Sleep was elusive though she thought it shouldn't be. She started to think about who might be trying to break in, but she immediately realized that such a chain of thought would not help her sleep. So she began doing the multiplication table aligned with her breathing and sure enough, that did the trick after a while.

When she woke up early on Sunday morning, Lauren considered going to church. She was an intermittent churchgoer at best, though she enjoyed going with Justin or the other Russells. They were Episcopalians, and she liked the time-honored ritual of the service. She liked how it changed through the year. There were a few things that she didn't particularly believe in, but that didn't bother her.

She liked how all the Russells had a down to earth attitude about religion. They didn't judge other people's faith or lack of it, or what churches people did or didn't go to, but she had seen that when things got rough for them, there seemed to be a bedrock beneath them.

She decided that a dose of church could be good for her today. She hadn't gone much in the past year, when Justin had rarely been in town. The service was what she more or less expected. No big deal, no earthshaking revelations, but it did her good to bask in something larger than herself and to share that with others. At the coffee hour, she fielded a lot of questions about when Justin would be back.

In the afternoon, Lauren walked Mickey over to the park for a training session with Sam. On the way there, she noticed that she and Mickey already had a closer rapport than they had before. Even though she hadn't trained him as much as she had intended to, they were more tuned in to each other. Sam noticed it too, as Lauren and Mickey approached her from across the park.

"Good work, Lauren, especially this week. Let me take him for a bit." Sam walked him around a little bit, and Lauren could see how he tuned in to Sam.

"Now let's up the ante, by going over there nearer the playground but still with some distance. You take him," Sam said.

Lauren was surprised that even though Mickey glanced over now and then at the children on the swings and climbing bars, he kept his attention on her. She rewarded him with little bits of dog treats that she had cut into tiny pieces and put in a small fanny pack.

Sam pointed to a German Shepherd being walked a bit further away. "Let's stay here in this area and see how Mickey behaves if the dog comes closer."

Lauren was pretty sure Mickey would go ballistic if the dog came within 10 or 20 yards of him. But she was wrong. The dog was being walked by a woman who seemed to take in the situation at a glance. She and the dog did come closer, but she diverted her dog's attention in a casual way so that when they walked by, the dog was watching the kids on the playground. Mickey bristled, but he didn't bark once.

When the dog and his person had passed, Lauren let out a big breath. "I'm amazed," she said. "Mickey's not that old, but he's like an old dog learning new tricks."

Sam laughed. "Let's walk him now in a quieter area to get his vigilance level down a bit, and then we'll see what other distractions we can find."

After a few more distractions, Sam decreed, "Enough. Let's go get a latte and bring it back here. Better yet, you and Mickey stay here and chill, and I'll go get them. You want a single tall one, right?"

Soon they were settled on their favorite bench overlooking the river. Mickey was glad to flop down and watch the birds on the water. "Here's my news," Sam began. "I've been helping the employees at Mike's Dog Place, and man I really want to take it over. Not as a manager but as the owner. It's a great space for training classes and private lessons. I don't think it would be all that expensive in terms of the real estate... My brother looked into it, and it looks like I could afford payments on it, that is, if my business went up some, and I'm sure it would." Her eyes sparkled.

"As for what the training business itself would be worth, frankly, I don't think it would be that much. When Ryan came by to help, we talked about it a little. He's no accountant, but he's no dummy either, and that geeky mind of his was helpful. I told him I was wondering if I could afford to take it over, and he confirmed my sense that it wasn't all that profitable a business. Seems like he and Mike were pretty tight, or else I don't know how he would have known some of the figures he tossed around. He did advise me to carry enough liability insurance."

Lauren asked, "Sam, did you have any discussion with Ryan about that theory of yours, that Mike might have been dealing?"

"No, I know Ryan from way back and I know he can be touchy, so I didn't want to push any buttons that might have been sore spots for him. Speak of the devil..." Sam pointed across the park to where Ryan was rapidly walking the Akita.

"I didn't know they'd be back so soon," Lauren said.

"I did... He said he'd give me a hand tomorrow. Let's go on now. Mickey's had enough stimulation for now."

"So have I," Lauren said. "More than enough."

NINETEEN

"Are you sure you don't want me to come back to Silvermine right now?" Justin asked on the phone.

Lauren sighed into the phone. "Honey, I'm not a damsel in distress. You are so close to coming home for good that I'd rather you just finish up your work in Fort Collins and get down here to stay. I really don't feel like there's anything you could do that I can't take care of one way or another, between bringing Spunky here and making sure the house is locked up tight. Oh, and I'm going to put a new latch between the greenhouse and the kitchen. I think I can install that myself and if I have any trouble I'm sure Don will help me."

"Well, okay... But I would be down there in a flash if you needed me," he said.

"I know that, and it makes me feel cherished. I'm really looking forward to getting on with our life together. I've been reading more about permaculture and I can see our piece of property turning into an incredible place. Did I ever tell you how much I love blueberries?"

"I don't remember if you told me, but I've certainly seen you pig out on them."

Lauren ignored his teasing. "I think I've spotted an area on the land that would be particularly good for them, near where the there's the hill."

"I haven't thought of anything else to put there. The other day I drew up a sketch map of where to put several different kinds of fruit trees."

"This is going to be so much fun," she said. "I love the idea of designing it all with you."

"Designing?" he asked. "How about digging the holes for the trees, laying the irrigation pipes, and all that?"

She laughed. "Oh, I'll give you a hand, when I'm not too busy at the library!"

After they wrapped up the conversation, Lauren felt a warm glow. It would be wonderful when Justin got here, not because he would protect her from anything, not because of the permaculture, but simply because she loved him.

She slept well that night, and Monday morning brought an interesting conversation at work. Grace was due to work at noon, and she came in a few minutes early to update Lauren on something that Paul had okayed her telling Lauren.

Grace could tell a good story as well as anyone, and she managed to drag this one out for a few minutes. But eventually it came out. "The police located Tammi and Tim, and sure enough, they were together. It's kind of amusing how they were found."

"How long are you going to keep me in suspense?" Lauren asked.

"However long I can," Grace laughed. "But seriously, they turned up when Tammi was pulled over for a speeding ticket here in Silvermine. She was driving Tim's car and he was with her. They were just coming into town late last night, so she is probably staying at her house now. It was just the speeding ticket that Paul told me, not anything else. He didn't pull her over but one of the other officers did and he told Paul."

"I was thinking of going downtown for lunch, but I think I'll just go on home and have a bite," Lauren said. "Just in case there's anything to see in the neighborhood."

There was a white car parked in Tammi's driveway, but even though Lauren ate her lunch in her living room, where she could see anything that happened, nothing did. When she got back from lunch, Grace gave her a querying look. Lauren just shrugged her shoulders.

But that evening, things got more interesting. Tammi knocked on her door, and when Lauren opened it, Tammi had the man with her. "Would you like to come over for some lemonade or something?" She asked. "This is Tim. I'd like to thank you again for your help and I want to update you on what's been going on. My sister stayed in Denver... she's better now but she had no desire to leave Denver for this so-called hick town."

"Sure," Lauren said. "Mind if I bring Mickey along? I'll leave the Rottweiler here."

"That would be fine," Tammi said.

Lauren locked up her house, something she wouldn't normally have bothered to do, and went across the street, Mickey tucked under her arm. She wasn't sure how he would take to either of them, especially to Tim, and she put a little bag of treats in her pocket in case she needed to chill him out.

Mickey didn't want her to set him down on the floor. He scrambled to climb up her legs, so she just put him in her lap as she sat in the armchair with a homemade lemonade in hand. At least, he wasn't growling or trembling, even when Tim sat down close to Tammi on the sofa. Lauren noticed that he put his arm around Tammi loosely but in a proprietary way.

"Did you wonder what happened to me?" Tammi asked.

"Yes, of course, especially after your sister took that hit that I assume had been meant for you."

Tammi made a face. "That's so awful. I just don't know what to think about it, who it could have been..."

Lauren said, "I guessed at the time that whoever hit your sister was the person who had killed Mike, and that he or she was afraid you knew too much."

"But I don't know a darn thing," Tammi said. Her voice rose as she said, "I've been over it all in my mind so many times. I just can't imagine what happened."

Lauren thought that Tammi seemed sincere. She had thought that before but wondered again if Tammi was a good actress. "Tammi, have you ever done any little theater?" As soon as she blurted out the question, it seemed too obvious that she was asking if Tammi would be good at faking her reactions.

"No... Why do you ask?"

"Well, I just wondered. I've been over it all a lot of times in my mind too." Lauren started to mention that a man had tried to break into her house one or two nights recently, but decided to keep quiet about that. The less she shared with suspects, the better, she reminded herself.

Tim said, "I've been talking it over with Tammi, and I think there must be something we don't know about Mike's life. You know, Lauren, I had been here that afternoon and evening, working with Mike on financials regarding opening another branch in another town. The numbers looked promising, and he and I were both in a good mood when I left here. The next thing I heard, he was dead. It doesn't make sense."

Lauren remembered hearing Tim whistle when he left Tammi's house that night. At least, this was an opening to talk about the business. "Have you discussed what to do with Mike's Dog Place?" she asked.

Tammi made a face. "That's a big pain. I can't run it by myself, and it's really not my thing. But it's my only financial asset. Besides, I want to be back in Denver." She glanced at Tim with a small smile.

Tim took over the chain of thought. "Lauren, you probably don't know that I'm an investor in the project. That was private information between Mike and me and of course Tammi. But even though I work in the pet supply retail market, I'm not a trainer. We'd like to sell to someone local if we could. I've got spreadsheets, and the business could be viable."

Lauren beamed. "Did you know that Sam has been helping out there?"

"Yes, I'm grateful to her," Tammi said.

Lauren couldn't let the moment go by. "Well, have you talked with her about taking it over?"

"You mean managing it? I'm not sure we could afford that," Tammi said, again glancing at Tim.

"No, what if she could buy it from you?" Lauren said.

Tim said, "I only met her for a minute when she stopped by to pick up Tammi for bowling, but I hear from Tammi that she is a dedicated dog trainer..."

Lauren said, "Yes, and a darn good one. I know because she trains my dog. I think she could make a go of it, though she might need financing. Her methods are different from Mike's, and she has quite a following around Silvermine. Do you have her phone number?"

"Yes, I have it. We'll call her soon," Tammi said.

"That's great. I'd love it if that worked out," Lauren said. "Not to change the subject, but I'm sure you've been thinking about this too... Do you have any ideas who could have killed Mike? Considering that you both could be suspects..."

Tim's eyebrows shot up. "The police have interviewed us both of course, but they were polite. Now you are calling us suspects..."

"I said you could be," Lauren countered. "Seriously, what do you think?" She deliberately left the question open ended.

"Of course, we've talked about it a lot," Tammi said. "I keep thinking that maybe nobody killed him, that he had just fallen from a heart attack or something. But my sister told me about the leg of lamb. I see it's not here anymore..."

"No, I told Paul about it and the police took it." Lauren thought about making a little joke about the famous short story where the meat is cooked, but decided that a story about a wife killing her husband wouldn't go over too well. She went on, "They probably put the key back by the back porch, so you might want to take it in."

"We already did," Tim said. "My opinion is that someone else must have come by after I left that Friday night, probably while the girls were out bowling or maybe when they were over visiting at your house. Whoever it was must have gotten into an argument with Mike, or maybe they came here with murder in mind. That's why I think there's something we don't know about Mike. I've known him for years, but chiefly as a pet store colleague."

Tammi looked over at Tim again. She said to Lauren, "It couldn't have been Tim. He would never do something like that. I think he's right that it must've happened after he left."

Lauren said, "I believe you both, but can you prove that neither one of you could have done it?"

Tim shifted his position and his voice was louder. "Are you doing the job of the police?"

"Not really," Lauren said. "It's just that my mind won't stop running around on what could have happened."

"What are your ideas?" Tim asked, with a trace of hostility in his voice.

"Well... I think you, Tammi, and I would have to be considered suspects. After all, I was home alone that evening, with just my dog." Absently, she snuggled Mickey closer to her. He woke up and sniffed around for a moment, before deciding there was nothing to lick and falling back asleep.

"So you think...?" Tim asked, in a more neutral tone this time.

"I know that I didn't come over to this house, so like you, I think someone else must have gone to see Mike. But who it could've been and what their motives might have been, I'm clueless," Lauren admitted.

They wrapped up the conversation in a reasonably friendly way, and Lauren went on home. Spunky jumped up on her, glad of her return. He weighed close to a hundred pounds, she guessed.

TWENTY

LAUREN FLOPPED DOWN onto her sofa, her mind racing. She was glad that Tammi and Tim had come back from Denver and she hoped they would stick around a while. When they were away, it was easier to think of them as villains, or at least as suspects. She had no idea if the police had moved beyond thinking of Tammi as the primary suspect. If she were to be found guilty, chances were she wouldn't get too heavy a sentence, as she would be seen as an abused wife.

But Lauren didn't think Tammi had killed Mike. Just because a lot of deaths were caused by immediate family members didn't mean this one was. Lauren had been thinking of Tim as a major suspect, but after talking with him this evening, she didn't feel that he had done it. What was that he said, that Mike had some part of his life that they didn't know about? That made sense, though Lauren did think Tammi might know something that she was overlooking or afraid to mention.

There was no point thinking about other suspects. She should just go to bed and let it all go.

The next day, Lauren wasn't due at work until noon. She slept in a little, but sleeping late wasn't really her thing. She took Mickey and Spunky down to the park for a nice long walk, jogging part of the way. For such tiny legs and a little body, Mickey could sure move fast. She ran along the trail by the river, and he had no trouble at all keeping up with her or Spunky.

She dropped both dogs off at Betty and Don's for the day, and then went home and had a leisurely brunch before getting ready for work. She walked to the library, enjoying the deep shade that the old trees provided for most of the way. It was already in the 80s in the sun, but the breeze made it pleasant.

Grace was working on the computer in the workroom, and the front desk was staffed. Lauren realized that this was a good time for the two of them to have a private talk. She went upstairs and told the woman at the desk that she and Grace would be having a conference but could be interrupted if necessary. Then she shut the door to the staff room, got herself a cup of coffee, and updated Grace on her evening with Tammi and Tim.

"Frankly, I'm clueless as to what happened," Lauren admitted. With a smile, she added, "I guess I'll just have to leave this one to the police."

Grace said, "That's a very good idea." She nodded deliberately.

Lauren said, "I'll probably still think about it some. It's just so perplexing. And the more I see Tammi and Tim, the less I think that either one could have done it. So if the police keep thinking it's her…"

Grace said, "My husband is no idiot. I'm sure he's exploring other options that he hasn't spoken about to me. Go talk to him at the police station if you want to."

"I just want to get the whole thing out of my skull," Lauren said.

"Hey, I heard something at church yesterday that I really like," Grace said. "Have you heard of paying it forward?"

"Yes, wasn't there a movie about that once?"

"There was, and it's become a kind of grassroots movement since then. Our minister preached his sermon about it Sunday morning. The idea is to do something nice for other people, often when something nice is done for you. You do it anonymously. He told us about one situation at a fast food place where literally hundreds of people kept a kind of chain going… When they drove up to get their order, they were told that the car in front had paid enough to cover it. Of course, by then that car was gone so they couldn't tell if it was anyone they knew or not. So like I said, they kept it going for a long time." Grace was practically bouncing with enthusiasm.

She went on, "Our family talked about it at lunch, and the kids were skeptical at first. But they got into it and came up with some really creative ways to pay it forward. I loved it that our minister challenged us to pay it forward as many times as we can this week. Then next week at the coffee hour, we'll talk about it."

"Let's see, you could pay people's overdue fines on their books and tell them that someone else had paid," Lauren suggested, laughing. "I think I'll try it too. I don't really see why I should wait to receive before I give... So today I'll do something. There is a related expression 'random acts of kindness.' I think that's what I'll do. Thanks, Grace, this makes me feel better. We all need some fun in our lives, and what's more fun than this?"

Lauren remembered something she had done for her youngest brother. She was in high school at the time, and he must have been in third grade or something like that. He was having a hard time making friends... Their family had recently moved, and he was in a new school. Lauren had decided to be his secret pen pal. She realized that he might recognize her handwriting, so she wrote him a postcard, using her left hand to print. That made it look more like kid's writing. When the mailman brought him the postcard, he couldn't believe it and showed it to everyone in the family, pointing out proudly that it was signed "your secret pen pal."

She sent him a postcard like that every couple of weeks for a few months, not stopping until he had plenty of friends at school. The last postcard explained that the secret pen pal was going away and wouldn't be writing any more. He was a little bothered by that, but he took it well.

She told Grace about it, laughing.

"See? You're a natural," Grace said.

As Lauren worked during the afternoon, her mind kept returning to things she could do. She thought of doing something for Paul, but discarded the idea because Grace would catch on. At one point, a girl asked her for help in finding dog stories in the children's fiction. She took extra time with the question, pointing several out to the child, and they had a nice conversation about dogs. But really, doing that was just part of her job even if she couldn't always take the time to be that thorough with everyone.

She thought of paying for something with cash, literally paying it forward. Could she do it for a customer at Don's auto shop? Not that she would pay hundreds of dollars... But she decided against it as she didn't want anyone else to know what she was up to. Well, what about a fast food place? She didn't usually go to them, but she could go home for dinner, pick up her car, and do it before coming back to finish the evening hours.

So she did that. She got herself a little bag of fries, and she gave the place an extra five dollars for the next car's order. As she munched on the fries while driving to the library, she was tickled at how good she felt. "Helping others is definitely a satisfying part of life," she thought to herself. She decided to keep on committing random acts of kindness and to keep a log of what she did in her journal.

After she got home from work, Don called. "I had a chat with one of my shadier customers today," he reported. "And I got an earful. If you'd like, I can bring the dogs over now and tell you about the conversation. Betty will stay here... Rosie is already asleep."

"Sure, you've got my curiosity going," Lauren said.

Don was soon settled in her living room. "When one of my customers came into the shop to get a part for his pickup, I thought he was a guy who could know what was going on around town. He's got a wicked sense of humor, but what he had to tell me wasn't funny at all. Evidently methamphetamine is seriously back in Silvermine. There was a time several years ago, before you were here and before Paul and Grace were here, when there was quite a bit. That got cleaned up, but now it's back in a big way."

Lauren had hardly breathed as Don said that. "I just don't get it... Why would anyone mess themselves up that way?"

"I hear that it's an amazing high, and I'm sure that's why people get onto it. I've never had any desire whatsoever to get near the stuff," Don said.

Lauren shuddered. "Can't people just get a life? Okay, okay, I know I'm being judgmental."

"The good news from this guy is that word is out that law enforcement is onto the situation. In any case, that's what I heard, whether it's gossip or more." He got up, gave Lauren his usual brotherly hug, and went home.

Lauren called the dogs in, made sure the house was secure, and got ready for bed. She could tell that her mind was racing, so she took her iPad to bed with her. Recognizing that reading about meth wasn't going to put her to sleep, she still couldn't help doing some web surfing about it. She read a few pages and then with a sigh, she turned off the iPad.

As she lay in bed, quite awake, she wondered if the meth in town would turn out to be connected to Mike's death in some way. After all, Sam had had that cockamamie idea that Mike was a dealer. Could he have been? She knew she had resolved to stop sleuthing about Mike's death, but her mind couldn't leave all this alone.

She tried praying, and gradually she became less wrought up. As she approached a state of sleep, Hercule Poirot popped into her mind. She didn't exactly see him, but she felt that he had a word of advice for her. "Librarian, be very careful," he said. "A dead librarian is completely useless."

That jolted her awake, and it was hours before she slept.

TWENTY-ONE

LAUREN AND GRACE were sitting side by side in the cramped workroom downstairs in the library, looking together at a spreadsheet Lauren had pulled up on the old desktop computer. Grace was frowning.

"I can find my way around a basic spreadsheet but this one is a bit much for me," she said.

"That's probably because I've got three different possible scenarios here," Lauren said. "The pale green column is the one I think to be most likely, the yellow column isn't as good but is barely workable, and the red column would be if the voters turned us down for any additional funding. I guess the spreadsheet is a little fancier than a usual budget... I'm really trying to get a handle on what we will be able to do."

The buzzer on the old phone sounded off, and Grace picked it up. "Why hello, Sam, yes, she's here. I'll pass her the phone in a moment, but tell me, how is it going at the Dog Place?"

Grace nodded as she listened. "Good... Here's Lauren."

Sam had never called her at work before. Lauren hoped that nothing bad had happened. "What's up?" She asked, a bit brusquely, skipping the social niceties.

Sam said, "Hey Lauren, sorry to disturb you at work. I'm just wondering if I can come by your house this evening to talk over the conversation I had just now with Tammi's friend Tim. Sounds like he's the money brains regarding Mike's Dog Place, now that Mike isn't here. He's playing hardball with me on the price, I think, but I wonder if you would have some time to help me work up a budget... I know you do that a lot for the library. Would you mind?"

Lauren laughed. "I was just sitting here working on a spreadsheet with Grace. Sure, I get off work at six..."

"Supposing I bring a gluten-free pizza over around 6:30? We could eat and talk and work for a while..."

"That sounds great! Mickey is over at Spunky's house, and we could walk over and get both of them after we work. Then I can show you how we are coming along. Also, I've got something else to run past you." She was thinking about the meth.

"Jane may come over too, as she might be involved in the project with me. I've already talked some with Ryan, when he came by yesterday."

"Whatever you want," Lauren said, wondering to herself if Jane knew anything about budgets and spreadsheets.

It turned out that she did. That evening, the three of them made short work of the pizza. Jane had also brought along her tablet, with a spreadsheet she had started during the day. Deftly, she typed in different numbers as they talked about whether Sam could afford the Dog Place.

Jane pushed her tablet back after a while. "You can do it, Sam, but there's not a lot of margin. I still think that Tammi's friend from Denver just doesn't get it that this isn't a big city and people won't pay big-city prices for dog services. If you could talk him down, it would be much better." She closed her computer, with an air of ending the discussion.

Lauren said, "I've got something else in mind that I wanted to run past you." Actually she had wanted to run it past Sam, and she wasn't going to stop since Jane was there also. "I've just heard that there's quite a lot of meth in town, and I'm wondering if it could have anything to do with Mike's killing." She watched both the other women as she spoke.

Sam nodded and Jane's face went blank. She seemed guarded.

Sam said, "You know that I wondered something like that myself, even more..."

Jane broke in, "I've got to get back to my kiddos. I'll leave you two to speculate. Sam, I'll email you my spreadsheet tomorrow. I want to play with it a little bit more first." She got up and left.

Lauren said, "That was abrupt. Do you think I offended her somehow by mentioning meth? You know her a lot better than I do."

Sam said, "Well, she's an odd duck. Don't forget that the night that we found Mike, she left really fast. I don't know what pushes her buttons but it seemed to me that something did."

Lauren said, "I really wanted to talk to you about what I heard about meth." She outlined what Don had told her he'd heard.

Sam let a long breath out. "Yeah, I know some about what's going on. Meth is like a virus, attacking people and then moving on to the people they know. I hope it doesn't catch Jane or Billy."

"Oh, maybe Jane left because she didn't want to talk about meth?"

Sam nodded. "She knows a lot of the same people that I do. I'm sure you know some of them too, from the library or whatever, but I don't want to get into listing a bunch of names. Not now, anyway. Say, speaking of the library, is there any kind of research I could do there about business prices in Silvermine?"

Lauren said, "I was going to surprise you with whatever I could find tomorrow. I work tomorrow night, and I think I'll take a look through the last year of the newspaper and some other Colorado sources, and see what turns up. I'll give you a call tomorrow after I get home from work... It will be a little after nine."

Together they walked over to Don and Betty's. Lauren walked Spunky and gave Mickey's leash to Sam. As they walked home in the dusk, Lauren was pleased by how well Mickey behaved with Sam. A group of six or eight teenage boys went by on their bicycles, and Mickey paid more attention to Sam than to them. That was real progress.

The next evening, Lauren found some figures regarding prices in different parts of Colorado. One article discussed real estate values and that would be useful, but the best one she found was in a Denver paper, evaluating the profitability of a local chain of hardware stores in different towns. It was clear that she had found some good ammunition for Sam in negotiations with Tim.

As she walked home, she decided she would phone Sam with the information. She had already emailed links to the articles, but she thought it would be fun to talk it over with Sam in person. She smiled to herself, being pleased that as a librarian she had been able to help Sam as a small business owner. This was a direction more and more libraries were going, and she would play it up next time she talked to the board.

She thought about how standing up to the board about improving the library had given her courage. It had helped her to do the random acts of kindness. She loved doing those.

It was just about dark as she walked through her historic neighborhood. They must have planted trees very early on, as some of them had such wide trunks. If she had been in some of the rough neighborhoods she grew up in, she would have been wary that someone could hide behind a tree like that and attack her. But here, despite everything that had been going on, she felt fine. If it wasn't safe here, was anywhere in the world safe? Well, no. She'd been sleeping well, and with Spunky in her house along with Mickey, she had heard no more sounds in the night.

She passed by a wide tree trunk, and was startled to hear a noise. She saw a tall man wearing a large black raincoat with the hood pulled up over the head. She thought what a strange thing to be wearing on a warm evening, in the split-second before he raised his arms and whacked her on the head with something that looked like a piece of lumber.

As Lauren heard him yelling at her, she fell to the sidewalk.

TWENTY-TWO

Lauren looked down. That was her body there on the sidewalk, all right, but she was above it, at about the height of the treetops. Surprised to see her body from this vantage point, she just accepted it. She was feeling okay. Not just okay... she noticed that there was no pain at all. Weird.

She basked in the calmness that enveloped her. It was all around her and it was within her too, with no separation between outside and inside. How lovely! It was dark in the neighborhood, and she savored the richly textured blackness around her. She had never noticed that darkness could be so alive, so full of sweet energy. It was like a soft black velvet cloak. She looked into the darkness, and off in the distance, higher up, there was an area of soft golden light.

As she put her attention on the light, she felt herself being drawn closer to it. The velvety black was still around her, but the golden area increased. She felt its warmth. Delicious. It felt like the very essence of love. She gave no thought to her body lying under the tree.

As the light encircled her, she saw her grandfather. He was standing just beyond a creek... she recognized the spot. It was in a park in Denver where her family liked to go. There were trees and grass and shrubs, but everything was more luminous than she remembered it.

"Grandpa, it's great to see you!" she said as she approached him. He didn't look much like he had in his last years. Instead of being bent over with wispy white hair, he was tall and vigorous. His hair was brown and he looked like a man in his prime.

"Lauren, my dear!" His deep brown eyes gazed intently at her.

She started to jump across the small creek, to go right up to him.

"No, wait," he said in a commanding tone.

"What?"

"If you cross the creek, you can't go back."

Lauren couldn't imagine any reason to go back.

Her grandfather said, " Sweetheart, you have things to do. Think of your life."

Dear little Mickey and her tall handsome lover Justin were instantly present in her mind. The Silvermine Public Library flashed by. So did Momo, her parents, and other family members. How much she loved them all, even more than she had normally been aware of. But this was so heavenly...

Grandpa said, "You will come back here when your work is done, I promise you."

She nodded. With a twinge of regret, she accepted her life back. And she felt herself moving away from him rapidly.

Lauren opened her eyes as her body was being loaded into an ambulance. She closed her eyes immediately and groaned as her head throbbed with pain.

The EMT said, "You're lucky that someone heard you screaming when you were attacked. We got here real fast. We'll have you at the hospital in no time."

"Uh huh," Lauren muttered.

Momo was with her, holding her hand. Lauren didn't open her eyes. How did Momo get in the ambulance?

"Momo! I thought you were still in Mexico!" Lauren said, noticing that she didn't have to move her lips to talk to Momo.

"Yes, my dear, we are. We've had a lovely time in Ajijic, and we're about to start the drive back home. We'll be back soon."

"Then how can we talk? Oh, is this being psychic?"

Momo laughed, and suddenly Lauren could see her. Momo was sitting on the patio of a cafe in Mexico, next to a wrought-iron table. A large striped umbrella came up out of the middle of the table and provided shade. There was a latte on the table in front of Momo and there was another one in front of Lauren.

She looked down and saw her own hands. She reached for the latte, had a delicious sip, and listened to the mariachi music coming from the other side of the block-long town plaza.

She said,, "I saw Grandpa and he told me to come back to my life. Did you see the Light too? Is that how come you can be in this world? This is another reality, isn't it?"

Momo smiled lovingly at Lauren. "My path has been a little different from yours. You just had what's called a Near-Death Experience... there are lot of books you can read later about them."

"Oh, yeah, NDEs, I ordered a couple of books on them for the library, but I haven't read them."

Momo went on, "Not that they will surprise you now, dear, but I'm sure you will enjoy reading them. I haven't had an NDE myself. After I was born, I didn't lose the connection with the world of Spirit in the way that people usually do. I remember seeing angels when I was a small child, and I've always been comfortable moving between the worlds. You might be more like me after this too, or you may go back more fully into so-called everyday reality. Time will tell."

Lauren said, "I love being with you like this. I want to keep doing it!"

She could feel the ambulance braking as it pulled up to the Emergency entrance of the hospital.

Momo said, " You're being pulled back into your world now. Any time you want, just call me and I'll come connect with you. And one bit of advice, Lauren..."

"Yes?"

"Don't be in a hurry to get right back into your everyday life, work and everything. Take your time, allow your experiences to change you."

"Of course!" Lauren said. "I will, absolutely." How could she not be affected by this?

The next thing she knew, she was waking in a room filled with sunshine. She could feel the brightness through her eyelids even without opening her eyes. Her head was bandaged and very sore, and her body ached in many places. She opened her eyes slowly. Oh, she was in a hospital room. Lauren felt woozy and not quite real... maybe she was full of meds.

Betty was sitting in a chair near the bed. "Hey Lauren," she said. "Good to see you waking up."

"Easier for you than for me," Lauren said. She hoped that didn't sound like a complaint when she simply meant it as an observation.

"Yeah, not much fun," Betty said. "We've all been worried about you..."

"I saw Momo," Lauren said.

Betty's eyes opened wide. "You did?"

"Yeah, she held my hand in the ambulance... I'll tell you later... hard to talk."

Betty said, "I think I'll go down to the nurses' station and tell them you woke up. Do you want some food?"

Food... Lauren hadn't thought of it but it sounded good. "A chocolate milkshake."

As Betty left, Lauren dozed off again. A doctor came in, quickly checked her eyes and a few other places on her body, and told her she'd had quite a concussion and some minor injuries. She'd be staying in the hospital for observation for a day or two longer. She couldn't really imagine moving around, so that was fine with her.

The next time she woke up, Betty was there with the milkshake. "I got an okay on this, and here you are." Lauren sucked eagerly on the straw. It was refreshing and tasty, but she was ready to doze off again before finishing it.

She went in and out of sleep as the day went on. Gradually, she began to think about things, a little at a time. She thought of Mickey. Betty had told her that he was staying with them and playing with Spunky, but that he wasn't quite himself without going home with Lauren last night. Too bad Justin wasn't back in Silvermine yet. She figured Betty or Don would have phoned him. She would ask Betty next time she felt up to talking.

Lauren let her thoughts go more fully to her little dog. Compassion for him flooded her as she saw how difficult things had been for him lately, from whatever it was that had him hiding under her bed to now when he couldn't be with her. She could feel his trembling in fear as if it were her own body.

She could even feel his barking as if it were her own body. That was different; she'd never barked. She could feel how sometimes he barked as a communication device, like the times he barked in the night, to warn away the intruder and wake up Lauren. She could also feel how there were times when he got so fired up that barking was his way of discharging energy. She'd have to talk that over with Sam.

Sam... thinking of her brought more of Lauren's life into her thoughts. That's right, there had been Mike's murder and everything that had followed from that. Lauren felt that she understood it all much better now. She dozed off again, reminding herself to scribble a few notes later.

When she did make some notes, she wrote, "Meth searching for Love. Terrible fear of loss." That captured the essence of one thing she needed to remember. There was so much more she understood now, about life, about herself. Amazing.

TWENTY-THREE

When Lauren woke in the late afternoon, she found a note on the bed that said Betty would be back soon. She stretched gingerly in the bed and took stock of her body. Her head felt like it was about double its normal size and as soon as she moved, there was pain. It wasn't terrible, but it got her attention and made her want to stay put. Her upper left arm was sore, maybe a bruise, and there were several other tender places she noticed, here and there on her body, all the way down to her left ankle.

Her awareness was much more back in her body, she realized. What with bandages and the bedding on her, she felt cozily wrapped up. It was odd to feel cozy in such circumstances, but she did. Was that the meds, or was it the aftermath of what had happened?

She set herself the task of remembering as much as she could. There was a note pad and pen on the bedside table. She nodded as she read the note about meth that she had written earlier, tore off that paper, and began making notes from the beginning.

Someone had attacked her as she was walking home from the library. She knew how the killer had felt, and she knew it was a man. It was the person who had killed Mike—a flood of insights about that would have to wait their turn for her full attention—and who had attacked Tammi's sister Marty. He had attacked her out of his terrible fear of being found out and sent to prison. She could feel the fear as if it was her own, right here and now, yet she was also somehow protected from being overwhelmed by it. Hmm, she could even feel his little tinge of regret as he hit her again and again. But she also felt his determination to do the job right and to leave her dead. She shuddered as she saw him run down the street and toss away the object he had been hitting her with. Was it part of a two by four? Whatever it was, it had landed in some bushes about half a block away. She'd have to tell Paul. She made a couple of notes on her paper. She still couldn't tell if it was a man she knew or not. Odd to be so in touch with someone's emotions without knowing who the person was.

But the attack was insignificant, really, compared to what had happened next. She had risen above her body and yet she had so absolutely been herself, Lauren, even outside of the crumpled body lying below her. What an incredible feeling that had been, and she felt it again now as her memories took her through the darkness, the golden light, and seeing Grandpa.

She thought about how she had almost jumped across the creek, eager to join her grandfather. So she had evidently been extremely close to death. She could be in that park now if Grandpa hadn't stopped her. She asked herself if she regretted that he had stopped her, and it was a yes-and-no sort of thing. Yes, it would have been unbelievably wonderful if she'd stayed there. She knew that now with all her soul, and she would never be afraid of death again. But she could also feel the overwhelming grief that her dog, her fiancé, and others would have endured, and she was glad that they wouldn't have to.

And really, for herself, she was glad to be back in physical reality, even aching in the hospital bed. She had enjoyed her life a lot before the attack, and now she loved it so much more. She loved the interactions with others with the possibilities for learning and growth. She loved the beauty everywhere in Silvermine, the mountains around it, and the world beyond. She loved making the library a better resource and how she served others in doing so. She'd always known that she liked to be of service through her library work, but now she felt it incredibly deeply. She laughed out loud as she imagined herself as a waitress wearing one of those old-fashioned black-and-white uniforms with a crisply starched white cap pinned to her hair, curtseying deeply to every person who came into the library, adults and children alike. Or would she look more like a maid in that getup? She didn't care.

And there was so much more she was grateful for. She thought of Mickey and of how Sam could teach her and Mickey to become even more unified in their lives through training. She thought of Justin and how the two of them were creating a life together that was fuller than their individual lives... she saw some of the permaculture projects they would create together on the land, including blueberries. That made her think of food, what a wonderful thing it was to experience delicious tastes. The occasional sadness she had felt that she was allergic to wheat transformed into no sense of lack at all, simply an awareness that she had a different palate of flavors to explore than most people.

Ahhh... she smiled at all she had to look forward to. Her body should heal up just fine in time, and even if she did end up with some limitations, they wouldn't matter in the big picture. She slowly stretched her body, feeling the pains but even more feeling the vitality that was even now running through her. She thought of doing a visualization about healing but realized that she already had something going on, the profound knowing that the healing was under way.

But there was one thing that came into her awareness that she had to do something about now... she needed to go to the bathroom. She looked around and saw a buzzer. She pushed it, and soon a woman in a uniform came in.

"I have to pee," Lauren said. "Can you help me to the toilet?"

"Sure, or do you want a bedpan like you did before?"

"I don't remember that, but I'd like to see how it feels to walk."

With the woman's support, Lauren got out of bed, walked across the room and into the bathroom, used the toilet, and walked back to the bed. She felt a ridiculous sense of triumph at her achievement.

She snuggled down into the cozy covers and closed her eyes. A little nap would be just the ticket.

When she woke next, the sun was down and she could see clouds tinged with sunset colors outside the window. Betty was reading in the visitor's chair.

"Hi," Lauren said.

Betty put her book down and smiled at Lauren. "How are you doing?"

"I walked to the bathroom," Lauren said, much like a child reporting on a new skill.

"Bathroom today, the world tomorrow!" Betty said.

"That's an amazing thought. Whatever happens is fine," Lauren said. "Betty, I had the most incredible experience after I was attacked." She told Betty a short version of it all, the velvety darkness, the golden light, and her meeting with her grandfather. She went on to the story of the conversation with Momo in Mexico.

"That's wonderful," Betty said. "I'd just as soon not go through what it took to get you there, though."

"Yeah, me either, but it happened and I'll be okay. Everything seems so different now... more majestic. I feel compassion for everyone, including the guy who whacked me..."

Betty said, "I'm not surprised. You've seemed downright happy all day, during the moments when you woke up for a bit, like when you had that milkshake."

"That was amazing," Lauren said. "Everything is amazing."

Betty said, "Are you ready for another amazing experience? I was just talking out in the hall..."

"Sure, whatever!" Lauren said, peering past the open door into the hall.

Don walked in, and behind him was Justin. Don stepped aside, and all Lauren could see was her fiancé.

He was wearing jeans and a t-shirt, and he was unshaven. His eyes were tired. Lauren had never seen him look more wonderful. He bent over to give her a kiss, and she loved his smell. The kiss was gentle. As he stood, they looked into each other's eyes and Lauren's future was glorious.

TWENTY-FOUR

Justin was home for good, earlier than he'd planned. He told Lauren that as soon as Don phoned him about her being attacked, he packed up everything and left, driving across the mountains like a madman. He said that he wouldn't have taken the time to pack but almost everything was in cardboard boxes so it didn't take long. "You scared me, honey! I had to come see you with my own eyes!"

Lauren said, "I'm a mess right now, huh?"

"A beautiful mess!"

They talked until Lauren's head began hurting more, seemingly from the concentration. Then Justin went home for the night, promising to collect Mickey on his way.

In the morning, Justin was there early, and Lauren's heart swelled to see him. His hair was still damp from the shower and he looked great, wearing jeans and a crisp blue shirt. The doctor let Justin stay while he carefully checked Lauren over. "The eyes can be affected by a concussion," he explained to them both, going on with more medical details.

She was pleased when the doctor said she could go home if she would take it very easy for a while. She and Justin both promised that she would. Lauren thought this was the first homecoming that wouldn't involve them rolling around on the bed right away. It would be quite a while before she'd be ready for that.

Justin had driven her little car to the hospital, and she stretched out as best she could across the back seat. He helped her into the house, through the living room which had his stuff scattered around, and right into the bed. Then he let Mickey in from the back yard.

The dog went crazy, barking and barking. Lauren could feel the barking reflecting his excitement at seeing her. He was saying something like, "I was so worried! Here you are! Life is good! You smell funny! You're here! You're HERE!" He jumped up on the bed and sniffed her through the covers up to her head—still sporting wrappings—and then he settled down right next to her head, looking up at Justin as if to indicate that there would be no discussion of his location.

Justin laughed. "You're fine there, little guy, I know exactly how you feel. In fact, that's a good idea." He stretched out on the bed on the other side of Lauren, and the three of them enjoyed being together again.

"I'm dozing off," Lauren said. "Don't be surprised if I do it a lot today. But go ahead and do whatever unpacking you want to... it won't bother me. Nothing could!"

"Except the way I left the living room?" Justin teased, as he went out to work on the task of moving back in.

Lauren fell into a deep sleep, dreaming of her grandfather. When she woke, her soreness bothered her more than it had before. Maybe she was off pain meds, or on lower doses. She grimaced as she climbed out of bed and tottered into the living room, where she sank down on the sofa. Mickey followed close behind.

Justin got her a cup of tea and some Arnica, a homeopathic remedy to help with bruises. He settled down next to her, his arm above her shoulders but putting no weight on her. "Can you tell me what happened, all of it?" he asked.

She told him everything, with frequent interruptions for his questions. When she got to how she had felt the fear that her assailant felt, she almost started crying for the man. Then she said, "Oh, I have a clue to tell Paul Johnson. Could you call the police station and ask him to come by?"

Justin said, "Sure, I'll make that call in a minute. But isn't it a paradox that you are feeling so sorry for the guy who tried to kill you and yet you want to get this clue to the police?"

Lauren said, "Yes, I guess it is, but life is paradoxical. I am sorry for the man, but I don't want him trying to do me in again, or anyone else. He's dangerous, obviously."

"Yeah, evidently," Justin said, embracing her so tightly for a moment that her bruises ached. "I don't know what I would have done if anything had happened to you."

Lauren thought to herself that plenty had happened to her, but she didn't need to pick at Justin's English at such a tender moment. "You know, it was your love—and Mickey's—that brought me back, more than anything. If I had died, that would've been okay for me, I know that now and I never did before. But I didn't want you and the others to go through what you would have."

Justin turned to look deeply into her eyes. "I can't begin to tell you what you mean to me. But since you're more psychic now, probably you know."

"Even without being psychic, I knew! Ain't love grand? I've been basking in it. But I think it's time for something to eat."

Justin rummaged around in the fridge and came up with a little assortment of foods. Lauren ate gratefully and then curled up in bed, Mickey right next to her, for another nap. As she dozed off, she heard Justin talking on the phone, setting up the date with Paul.

Soon, Paul came over. She told him where the attack weapon might be found. "I'm quite sure it was thrown into a large clump of lilacs about halfway down the block from where I was attacked."

Paul made notes as she talked. "Did you see it?"

"A little bit when I was attacked, but later I had a kind of movie running in my mind about how the man took off down the street. I saw him tossing something like a two-by-four under lilac bushes in front of an old two-story white house. I don't know the people who live there, but come to think of it, it looked like the house needed painting."

"That will be easy to check out, and we'll do it right away. Do you remember that I stopped by your room in the hospital, when you were still going in and out of consciousness?"

"No, I don't recall that, but I don't remember much from then."

"You muttered something about meth, do you remember what that was about?"

Lauren's eyes moved as she tried to access the memory. "Paul, I have the weird feeling that whoever was hitting me was on meth. I don't think I sensed it at the time of the attack—I remember being astonished and concentrating on avoiding the blows, not that I was very successful there."

"On the contrary," Paul assured her. "You may have saved your life by evading some of the worst blows. You were screaming too, according to the people who called 911. They didn't see you but they sure heard you."

"I don't remember screaming. I barely remember the attack," Lauren said.

"More may come back to you, and if any significant details do, please call us right away. That reminds me... Grace checked out one of the library's books on your card and asked me to bring it along for you." He gave a paperback on near-death experiences to Lauren.

"And I've got something else from Grace for you," he said with a smile. He stepped out onto the front porch and came back in with a large piece of pink poster board. In the middle it said, "GET WELL SOON! WE MISS YOU!" and there were dozens and dozens of signatures in a rainbow of colors. People of all ages had signed it. As Lauren scanned the names, she recognized most of them.

"It's weird but I can feel the love in those signatures," she said. "And I can sense so much about each person, just looking at those. I don't mean like handwriting analysis, it's just that they have put something about themselves into signing their names. Does that make sense?"

"Sounds like you will be giving Momo a run for her money," Justin said.

"Maybe. It's just that I can tell so easily now how love is the texture and substance of everything. Oh, Paul, that's part of what I might have been muttering about in the hospital when I mentioned meth. I remember somewhere in all that, I had an awareness that meth users are hungry for love."

Paul's eyebrows went up. "They are trying for it in entirely the wrong way."

"Yes," Lauren agreed. "They are. But I can feel the yearning in them. Oh, by the way, I had an odd idea about Mike. I wondered if he might have been selling meth. In a way, he had the perfect setup. But I've also noticed that I really don't care who killed him. I think my sleuthing days are done. That's your job, not mine."

Paul said, "That's good."

TWENTY-FIVE

Lauren healed steadily at home, though her bruises were multi-colored before they began fading. She was stiff and sore, and the emotional high she'd been living in at first began to fade.

"I'm glad to see you grumpy," Justin said to her one morning as she got up complaining about her aches and pains. "For a while there, it seemed like you were going to be blissed out permanently."

"I wouldn't have minded that," she said, wincing as she slipped into culottes and a blouse. She sat on the bed to put her shoes on. "Believe me, it would have been just fine. But I've been reading about the aftermath of NDEs, and it seems that ups and downs are pretty normal. Some people get depressed that they are back in this life. At least, I haven't had that."

Justin sat beside her on the edge of the bed, and took her lightly in his arms. "This hurt too much?"

"Nope, not for a minute... Say, how does it feel to be back in Silvermine to stay?"

"Great! I'm really pleased to be home. Can't wait to go out to the land with you and show you some more permaculture ideas I've been mulling. I want to start planting some trees soon. My folks send their love, by the way... they'll be home from their vacation soon. Best of all is being with you, Lauren." He took her hand tenderly and nibbled his way up her arm, giving her air-kisses above the bruises.

She leaned over and gave him a small kiss on his cheek. How good he smelled! She nuzzled into him for a little bit, but it really did hurt so she moved away.

"I have a doctor's appointment this afternoon, right? Anything else planned?" she asked.

"I'll take you to that, and then we are going to Betty and Don's for dinner, right from there. That's all that's scheduled but Sam called while you were still asleep this morning, and she'd like to come see you."

"Good, okay if I invite her for lunch today, even if you've still got to be the chef?"

"Yeah, I'd like to see her," he said. "I'll just do grilled cheeses and a salad, no problem. We're not taking anything to my brother's tonight."

"Okay, I'll call her."

Justin settled down in the dining room which had rarely been used for eating. He was in the midst of turning it into a home office, and lumber for bookshelves was lying next to where it would soon be put up. He had left Fort Collins so abruptly that he had a couple of reports to finish up.

Lauren stretched out in the recliner for a while, Mickey on her lap. She wasn't sleepy at all, and she went into a place in her mind she'd been before, when she'd had the conversations with Hercule Poirot and with Margaret and Karen. Now she understood that frame of mind much better. Her body became more relaxed and she was paying less attention to it. The persistent aching from various spots around her body faded into the background. If she didn't pay attention to the aches, they were hardly even there. What a relief.

Her mind felt sharp and clear... no wonder this space was often called the inner world. That's what it truly was, she knew that now, in a vivid new way. She let her mind drift to what it had felt like when she'd been enveloped by the vibrant black after she was attacked, and she could feel it much more fully than when she had told the story to people. She stayed with the velvety black for a while, and then went on to the golden Light. Amazing how great the Light felt... it still surprised her how palpable the love was. Tears of gratitude came to her eyes.

And then, she saw her grandfather again. He smiled at her across the creek... this time he was further back from the creek and it looked like he was doing some tai chi. He'd never done that during her childhood. She waved at him, surprised and happy that she could see him again. She wondered if she would be able to keep the connection going. That would sure be nice, but she didn't have the sense of wanting it in a way that made her attached to what happened. Ah, a nice Buddhist touch. Non-attachment made more sense now.

Her attention drifted back to her body on the recliner with Mickey. He was dozing, and she could feel his contentment. He'd been really happy when Justin came back to stay. She sent Mickey a little love-thought and he stirred in his sleep.

What did she want to think about now? Well, it was time to look at the insights she'd had about Mike during her NDE? She remembered she had learned some things about Mike that she needed to look at. Even though she had vowed not to be involved again, this needed to be finished up for her to let go of it.

"Okay," she said inside herself. "Mike."

Immediately she felt rigid and uptight. It was an inner feeling, and even though she knew it didn't belong to her, she noticed that her muscles were suddenly aching more as she lay there.

"Umm, not so good," she said to her inner self. "Let's try to do this without the special effects."

Her body relaxed again. Cool!

"Okay, what do I need to know about Mike? Please show me, but give me a bit of distance from it." Who was it that she was asking this of? Her inner self, whatever that was... food for thought later.

She felt as though her iPad was being held in front of her. On it, she could see a video playing. It was so real that for a moment she wondered if it was an actual home movie that Tammi or someone had taken.

She watched Mike as he sat at his desk at Mike's Dog Place. His office was a small room off the reception room, and he had the door shut. He was concentrating on the desktop computer in the office. She didn't know what it was he was examining, but she sensed how tight he was. But it wasn't just his body. There was a tightness in his aura.... Aura? How woo woo was she getting? But she was aware that he lived totally with a tightness around him.

She turned her attention to what he was doing on the computer. He was opening a spreadsheet, but he seemed more furtive than she'd expect from something so mundane. The file had a password and she saw what it was as he typed it in. It was pretty long, but she recognized it as his last name and then his street address with the house numbers backwards. Then she found herself looking at the spreadsheet closely. It was a simple one, and it took her a moment to realize it didn't seem to have anything to do with dogs. It was a list of first names, with dates and amounts of money in columns.

Her mind went back to the idea that Sam had raised, that Mike might be selling meth. Would he keep track of it on a spreadsheet? How odd. That would explain the password though. She noticed that her stomach was getting tight as she went between watching the action as if on her iPad and being in the scene.

"Easy," she said to herself. "I want to watch this like a film. What else do I really need to understand?"

The view zoomed in on the list of names. Most of them she didn't know, but there were a couple of names she recognized. One of them made her gasp. "Really?" she muttered to herself. "That's too bad."

Then she was looking at Mike and Tammi together, seeing how hard Tammi had tried to make life good for Mike. She understood now that Tammi had a deeply loving nature, and that she had done her very best for Mike. Lauren wondered in passing how many abused wives were like that, loving so much that they forgave too much. Well, Tammi's life would be better now. Lauren wasn't sure quite what was going on between Tammi and Tim but she felt the love and respect between the two of them.

Lauren thought to herself that she had underestimated Tammi, and she wondered how many other people in her life she had underestimated. Like her parents... she went into a reverie about her childhood with them, seeing some events in a new light. That felt good. She hadn't told them yet about her NDE, wanting to do that in person. She'd emailed with her mom since coming home from the hospital, but only with a few medical details and that she was getting better.

She stretched in the recliner and noticed her body again. Mickey hopped down and went to see Justin in the home office. She opened her eyes... Nope, that was too fast. She closed them again and reviewed everything that had just happened. It was quite a pleasant surprise that she could go see her grandfather, if only from a distance, but the real surprise had been what she'd seen on the spreadsheet and what that had made her understand. It made her feel sad, but many things fell together now.

TWENTY-SIX

WHEN SAM ARRIVED, Lauren was ready for a talk. She wondered for a moment if Justin's presence at lunch would inhibit Sam, but she decided they'd play that by ear. After all, didn't everyone in town know each other's secrets from high school and beyond?

"Hey Samantha! Long time no see," Justin said with a big smile.

Sam gave him a bear hug, Mickey jumping up on both of them for attention. Sam picked him up and talked to him. He accepted being put down, and the people sat down for lunch.

"So, girlfriend, you got attacked big time," Sam said. "I heard that, and you sure look like it. But I also heard that you had some sort of life-changing experience..."

Lauren wondered what Sam would make of her story. She couldn't go around censoring what she told people. She'd just give Sam a short version and see how she reacted. She passed the salad to Sam.

"Yeah, I had an NDE, a near-death experience."

Sam's eyebrows shot up. "Really? Did you see the light and all that?"

"Yep, sure did." Lauren took it that Sam was interested and so she launched into the story. She never tired of retelling it, as it made her feel so good. Justin had told her that he might someday get tired of hearing it, but he figured it would take at least a few dozen iterations, and she was nowhere near that.

Sam was tough minded as ever, and she asked a bunch of pointed questions. Lunch was over by the time the subject was exhausted. As they sat in the back yard with fruit and coffee, Lauren turned the conversation in another direction.

"Sam, I seem to be a little more like Momo now, more able to pick up things that I wasn't aware of before. And it seems to me that your idea that Mike could have been dealing meth has a lot of merit. I can feel how it could be true, from an inner vision I had."

Sam nodded. "It makes sense to me too." She turned to Justin. "I remember that you had left town for college when there was that big meth episode here. Did you know about it?"

Justin shook his head. "Not much. I remember Don telling me that a lot of people he knew had tried it, and that some got hooked, and that some got in trouble with the law, but they were all younger than I was. Then later Don told me it had been cleaned up."

Sam said, "That's accurate. But it's being cooked in town again now." She glanced at each of them, then went on. "I'm quite sure that Mike was selling it, from what I've been hearing. My dog training business has picked up some clients of Mike's, and a couple of them told me essentially the same story... They both said that Mike casually mentioned to them that he could get them some if they wanted it. Neither one of them did, and they thought it was strange that Mike had mentioned it."

"Have you told Paul this?" Lauren asked.

"Yes, I saw him at the grocery store yesterday and so I had a few words with him next to the meat section. He wasn't surprised, I could tell."

Lauren said, "You know how involved I've been with sleuthing, but that has really changed after my NDE. It seems like I've been trying to make everything okay all my life, and this is going to sound strange but I don't even care if the murder is solved. Well, I do care but not like it's my problem... it's up to law enforcement and not to me. What I really care about is in my life, Justin, Mickey, family, you and my other friends, and the library. It's a relief. I got it that everything was okay all along, and I never saw that before. I'm not condoning murder or cruelty, but there's a much bigger picture, and that's the level where everything is all fine."

Justin was watching her intently. "That's the clearest that you've said that."

"Yeah, that's cool," Sam said. "I've gotta say I thought you were a bit obsessive about trying to solve the murders, this one and the ones that happened before."

"Still, I think I know how Mike got killed." Lauren said, "I think someone went to his house while Tammi was out bowling with you. Something happened—probably an argument—and I'd guess that Mike threatened or even attacked the other guy, who picked the leg of lamb up off the counter where it was thawing. He used it in self-defense and accidentally killed Mike."

"You're saying it was a guy?" Sam asked.

"Yes, because we know it was a man who attacked me and Tammi's sister Marty. I think it was the same person."

"Who?" Sam and Justin asked in the same breath.

"I don't know who. I felt his emotions, like his fear of being caught, but I'm not at all sure who it was."

Sam took a deep breath and spoke directly to Justin. "When meth was popular back then, I was one of the people who tried it. Man, I could have gotten onto it so easily. The two times I used it were just friggin' wonderful. I loved it."

Justin looked at her with the characteristic respect that Lauren loved in him. "Yeah, I heard then that you were one of the people in that circle. But you managed to break away."

"I did, after one of my best friends fried her brains bad. Didn't tell you that, Lauren, I didn't want to get too much into my memories."

Sam leaned over and picked Mickey up. "Hey, Mickums, little guy, it's easier being a dog, honestly, it is." Mickey snuggled into her lap. Sam looked at the others and shrugged. "Wish I was one myself sometimes."

"That's why you're so good with dogs," Lauren said. "Say, I'm walking around the house and yard now. Let's do another training session with Mickey one day soon, in the back yard."

"Excuse me," Justin said. "I'd better go back to my report." He grabbed another cup of coffee and disappeared into the home office, closing the door.

Sam watched him step out. "You're hooked up with one of the few men I've ever imagined being with. When he was in high school and I was in middle school, I had a crush on him for just about the whole year."

Lauren was astonished. "I never knew that."

"No, I never told anyone but Momo, and she keeps secrets. I don't think he ever knew, but if you feel like telling him, I don't care any more. I'm really comfortable with myself now as a loner. I doubt I'll ever have a permanent partner, it's just my nature to need a lot of solitude, with dogs of course. But enough about that... I have some great news about the Dog Place."

"What?"

"I've been talking with Tammi and Tim, and we're going to be able to work a deal. I was worried that they would ask too much, but it turned out that Tim was just protecting Tammi's interests and when he saw the figures you found, he was fair about lowering the asking price. With the help of my family, I am going to buy out Tammi's share of Mike's Dog Place and I'll rename it Samantha's Dog Place. My family is being great about how I pay them back. Tim was an investor in the place with Mike, and I'm going to pay him a thousand bucks up front, sort of as a good-faith deposit, and he's going to stay on as an investor with me. He'll help me get set up with wholesalers in pet supplies too, and I'll turn one of the rooms into a shop for leashes, dog food, dog toys, stuff like that. There are still details to work out, but we all agree it's going to work. I think we can do it pretty fast and the place won't have to close at all. I'm going to order a big banner for the front of the building this afternoon that will say, 'Under New Management!' and get my name up there."

Lauren jumped up from the table, smiling broadly, to give Sam a hug. "That's wonderful, Sam!"

She sat back down quickly, noticing her soreness. Mickey jumped up into her lap.

"Another cool thing," Sam said. "There's a small apartment on the side of the building, with a kitchen and bathroom. It was a door that goes into the kennels. Mike just used it for storing supplies, but I'm going to paint it and fix it up and move in. That way, I'll be right there whenever I'm needed. You know how I've often boarded dogs in my apartment. This is way better. I can't wait!"

They talked about her plans for the place, Lauren suggesting that Sam could do programs on dog training at the library sometime, one for children and one for adults. They had other ideas for how to get the word out that Samantha's Dog Place would now be a place of positive dog training methods only.

Lauren said, "Before we stop talking about dogs..."

"As if that will ever happen!" Sam said.

"Yeah, you're right. Anyway, I wanted to ask your opinion about what scared Mickey so much the night of Mike's murder. Remember, I came home from work and Mickey was hiding under the bed? Momo told me she saw a guy coming up on my porch and staring in at Mickey, who'd been barking. But then later that evening, after you picked up Tammi, he wouldn't stop barking. I've just been wondering about that."

Sam said, "So didn't you say that you are more psychic now?"

"I guess so, but I haven't really got that sorted out yet."

"I am no psychic, never will be," Sam said. "But with that bond you have with Mickey, I bet you could just ask him. You might get some clue about what happened."

"I'll try that," Lauren said. "And Momo should be back from Mexico any day now, so I can run whatever I get past her."

"Cool," Sam said. "Now, how about if I take your little dog for a run down to the park and back? Bet he'd like the exercise, and I would too."

Lauren nodded and Sam grabbed the leash from the hook by the front door. Mickey jumped up, and the two of them took off at top speed.

Lauren flopped down on the bed, worn out but not sleepy. Her mind turned to the evening when Mickey had barked as she was reading. Probably the barking was caused by the same person who had come up to the porch and intimidated Mickey that afternoon.

She sighed. She hated to accept it, but she had to. Who else but Ryan walked so much in the neighborhood and had business dealings with Mike?

TWENTY-SEVEN

Lauren waited until she and Justin were having dinner at Betty and Don's to voice her theory. Rosie had already gotten down from the table and gone to play with her toys in the back yard when Lauren said, "I hate to bring this up, but I think Ryan may be the one who killed Mike and attacked me and Tammi's sister. I don't have proof but he fits the picture." She picked up her fork but didn't have the heart to eat.

Don said, "Could be. That night that we were eating here when a neighbor brought Rosie home, I was about to tell you something but never got to it. Ryan was arrested twice just after high school, both times on drug charges. One was when that meth ring was here, and I don't know about the other. He spent some time in jail. I heard he stayed away from drugs after that."

"Of course," Justin said. "Colorado is a three-strikes state. If it's him, he's looking at a nasty prison term. Not that killing Mike and attacking you and Tammi's sister wouldn't be serious in their own rights."

Lauren said, "I'd hoped that among you three, someone would be able to explain why my theory didn't hold water."

"Nope, I think you may have nailed it," Justin said. "But will there be enough evidence to charge him? I guess we'll find out soon enough."

Lauren couldn't eat. She sipped listlessly on her wine. "I thought we were on good terms," she said. "He took good care of the library computers, and I'd chat with him then and sometimes when I saw him walking around the neighborhood. Why would he think he had to kill me? Oh, wait a minute... I just remembered something I picked up about when I was being attacked. I actually did feel a bit of regret coming from the man who was hitting me, when I relived it later on."

Justin said, "I hope you don't end up with PTSD and keep reliving it."

"I think I might have a bit of that," Lauren said. "It does keep cropping up. But I also have such vivid memories of my NDE, so it's quite a mixture."

Justin looked at her with concern. Lauren thought how soulful his eyes were.

"Wait just a minute, everybody," Betty said. The others all looked at her, surprised at her firm tone of voice.

Betty continued, "I for one am not convinced that it was Ryan. Yes, he walks around town a lot. Yes, he was tight with Mike. Yes, he had a history with meth. But... it just doesn't feel right."

Lauren said, "I don't think anyone is going to feel right, because murder never feels good. If it's anyone we know, it's going to bother us, don't you think?"

"As a general philosophical comment, I agree with you," Betty said. "But I am being specific. I've known Ryan a long time and I simply don't get the feeling that he did it. And this has nothing to do with his having had that crush on me years ago. It's how my gut feels right now."

"I hope you turn out to be correct," Lauren said. "But who could it be if not him? I am convinced it was a man, since it was a man who attacked Tammi's sister and me."

"I don't know anything more," Betty said. "This is a gut feeling, a strong one. I wish I was like Momo and could get more information. No, wait a minute... now I'm seeing a picture. It's Ryan arguing with another man. He's really mad. That's all I can tell."

Don asked, "What does the other man look like, honey? Where are they?"

Betty put her hand on her forehead. "I'm sorry, I just don't see more than that. I can feel that Ryan is really furious, that's all."

"This is interesting," Lauren said. "Betty, if you close your eyes and look at your image of Ryan, do you get any more details?"

"I'll try it," Betty said, closing her eyes. "It's dark. They are on a porch or someplace like that. The other guy is sitting in a chair and leaning over. I don't see his face. He's wearing a short-sleeved plaid shirt, and he's pretty thin. His hair is brown and he could use a haircut. The feeling coming from him is... well, it's despair, I'd say."

Don nodded at Lauren and said, "Honey, anything else?"

Betty shrugged. "It's all kind of a jumble, but I think I hear him talking to Ryan in a low tone of voice. He doesn't sound angry, not like Ryan."

She stretched and opened her eyes. "That was so vivid. It was really like I was there watching. But I don't know what to make of it."

"Thanks for doing that," Justin said. "I'm sure it's not easy to have your gifts."

"I don't usually feel like they are gifts," Betty said. "Most of my life, I've hated it when this happens. This was clearer than some things I've seen, but not like that terrible time in high school. Still, I wouldn't place any bets based on this little scene."

Don rose from the table. "Let us know if you get anything else, even if it doesn't make a lot of sense, okay?" He turned to Justin and Lauren and said, "You both know that every now and then something she has seen turns out to be very real. I haven't had a chance to tell you that last week she warned me about a red-headed guy with a birthmark on his cheek. Darned if a guy fitting that description didn't come into my shop and try to steal some of my hand tools. You just never know. Well, enough said! Strawberries and ice cream, anyone?"

Lauren's appetite returned when she saw the strawberries, big luscious ones from the garden. "Justin and I are planning to plant blueberries out on the land. We'd better make sure to do a good large strawberry patch too."

"Why are you thinking permaculture and how will that be different from just regular gardens?" Don asked.

Lauren could tell that Justin was about to launch into a fervent permaculture lecture. He must have realized this wasn't the moment for it, as he just said "It's important now more than ever to design gardens and landscape in harmony with the climate and terrain. Lauren and I will be drawing up some plans soon, and you'll see how they will fit really well into the land."

As the evening ended, Lauren felt drained, as she usually did by the end of the day these days, but she also felt a glimmer of hope. She really didn't want it to be Ryan who had attacked her. But who could it be if not him? No, stop, she told herself. Justin drove home and she got ready for bed right away. He lay down beside her for a few minutes, but she was still too sore for much cuddling. She barely noticed when he got up and went out to his office.

She woke the next morning at first light, Justin sound asleep on his side facing her and Mickey curled up at her feet. She lay there feeling her aches and pains but also with a quiet happiness. Since her NDE, everyone seemed more glorious to her, even though life also seemed more complex. She remembered a quote that the line between good and evil goes through every human heart, or something like that, from Aleksandr Solzhenitsyn. She could sense how the great patterns of life ran through every person and dog. She wondered about other animals, too. Well, cats certainly... but she wasn't going to make a judgement call on whether cockroaches could experience love and hate!

She felt more accepting of the possibility that Ryan might have committed the murder and the two attacks. She could see a lot of good in him, but if that wasn't all, well then it wasn't. He was human.

What about Betty's gut feeling last night that Ryan wasn't the killer? Lauren had been glad to hear it, but she didn't have such a feeling herself, one way or the other. She tried to set aside everything she'd been thinking about and see if she did have any kind of gut feeling about what had happened and who had done it.

Nope, she didn't. Evidently her NDE had not given her the gift of predicting the future or even of being more like Momo or Betty. She consoled herself that one gift she had received was the certainty that life was more glorious than she had ever realized. She thought to herself that she could at least predict that the future was going to be glorious.

She could predict that her own increased compassion was likely to continue, and that she would keep on enjoying and celebrating the majesty of each person's uniqueness. With that grand thought, she got up and took her shower, feeling glad that she could do more simple tasks every day. One of these first days, she would go into the library for a few hours.

TWENTY-EIGHT

LAUREN SPENT THE morning doing simple projects around the house, while Justin worked in his home office. She was getting used to his presence. Since it was better not to distract him when he was working, she picked up the cordless when it rang and answered it out into the backyard.

"Are you sitting down?" Grace asked.

"No, I'm in the yard. If I'd better sit down, you must have something big to say... Okay, I'm sitting, go ahead."

"The meth ring has been busted and arrests made."

"Holy cow," Lauren said. "Tell me everything you can."

"It's public knowledge now... was on the radio news already," Grace said. "I didn't have any advance knowledge myself. I'm relieved that the main baddies are in jail, the ones who were doing the cooking and the bulk of the selling."

"Geez, I wonder if Mike would have been arrested if he'd been alive."

Grace asked, "He was dealing?"

"It seems like it from what Sam heard. A couple of her dog training clients who used to work with Mike told her he'd offered to sell them some. Also, I had a kind of vision the other day that he had a spreadsheet on his computer at work listing some of his customers. I even saw the password of the file."

"Paul would be interested in that," Grace said. "He's in the office now... why don't you call him?"

"Sure," Lauren said. "Thanks for the news."

Justin came out of his office asked her what that was about, so they talked a few minutes before she went in the living room to call Paul. She told him what Sam had said and also about the spreadsheet, emphasizing that she had only seen it in her imagination. She didn't go so far as to say she had recognized two of the names on it.

He was interested. "We need to check the computer right away. We'll get right on it. I expect there will be a staff member at the Dog Place, taking care of the dogs."

"Tammi's in town," Lauren said. "I heard her out in her front yard earlier this morning. By the way, congratulations on catching the meth people."

"A lot of teamwork went into that," Paul said. "It was a great relief."

"Think it will help you with solving Mike's death?"

"We'll see," Paul said, with a ring of finality in his tone that Lauren understood. He wasn't going to tell her anything.

She and Justin had lunch together and then she took her now-obligatory nap. Grumbling to herself about still being tired, she admitted that she felt a lot better after the nap. When she went back to work at the library, she might miss those naps at first.

She was up and puttering around when the phone rang again. To her surprise, it was Ryan, asking if he could come by and talk with her and Justin.

"Sure," she said. "Sam is coming by in an hour. Want to come then too?"

"Will do," Ryan said. "Thanks."

"Umm, thank you yourself," Lauren said, wondering what he had on his mind. Evidently he hadn't been arrested... unless he was already out on bail.

Lauren sat down and thought hard, but thinking didn't do her any good. What a puzzle. She called Sam and asked her to come over earlier so she could tell her some news. She asked Justin if he could quit work for Ryan's visit and he said of course. A little tidying up of the house, and throwing the ball for Mickey to chill him out filled up her time.

Sam had been working at the Dog Place and hadn't heard about the meth busts. "Who did they get?" she asked.

"No idea," Lauren said. "But here's the other part of my news. Ryan called and asked if he could come over. He'll be here in a few minutes. I mentioned that you would be here and that was fine with him. I really wonder what is on his mind, and it's interesting that he's not in jail."

Sam whistled. "Glad I'm here for the next chapter. Say, I got my Dog Place sign ordered. It will be larger than Mike's sign, without the cartoon he had, and my name will be easily visible as you drive by. Ben and the other employees are working and they will all continue with me. Today I've been cleaning out that apartment, with Tammi's okay. She's being really nice about my taking the place over before we get all the paperwork done on the sale... it must be a relief for her. The apartment had so many cardboard boxes and other stuff in it that I thought it was tiny, but when I got all that out of there, it's really a good size. It's a one-room studio with a small bathroom. The kitchen is an alcove with cabinets built in, and the stove and fridge are clean. I doubt Mike even made a cup of coffee in there. I'm going to move in as soon as I can!"

"I heard all that," Justin said, coming out of his office and closing the door. He was using the door to signal whether he was working or not. He made some coffee and they speculated about what Ryan would say.

Ryan knocked quietly, and Justin went to the door. Lauren was sitting on the sofa where she could watch Mickey's reaction to Ryan coming in without his dog. Mickey had sniffed noses and butts with the Akita a number of times, and he didn't show much reaction to Ryan coming in, just one quick little bark.

"Coffee?" Justin asked.

"Uh, sure," Ryan said awkwardly, staring at Lauren. She had deliberately left off her head scarf and worn short sleeves, so her scars, scabs, and now-multi-colored bruises were evident.

"You're quite a sight," Ryan said to her. His tone was dry and Lauren couldn't read his emotions.

"Yeah, you should have seen me before. I'm over the worst of it," she said.

"I heard you were attacked on your way home from work," he said.

"Yes," Lauren said, glaring at him slightly.

He didn't react to that. "Well, I guess you wonder why I'm here," he said, looking at each of them in turn. "Paul and I thought I should tell you a few things..."

Lauren felt her heart beating faster.

"Sam probably remembers that I had a couple of drug busts right after high school. I did time and that scared me, so I cleaned up, haven't even had weed in several years."

He was looking right at Lauren as he spoke. She nodded, her eyes wide.

"When Mike started the Dog Place, he hired me to set up the accounting software on the desktop computer in the way he wanted it, which was with some categories for income that would be hard to spot, hidden deep in cost of goods sold. He had me do anti-virus work too, but he was more worried about someone tracking him with keyloggers than about getting a virus from web surfing. I don't think he ever used that computer for casual use. He was all business. He would only pay me cash and he told me not to tell the computer company I work for that I was doing that for him."

Ryan cleared his throat. "One evening, I was working there and I was tired... Malinda and the kids had been sick the night before. Mike was doing other things around the place, but he noticed when I went to get some more of the vile coffee their machine had. He offered me something to boost my energy. When I asked him what it was, he just smiled and offered me a white capsule. I accepted it and after a while I got a euphoric rush. I remember thinking that it had to be meth. I hadn't had any in years and it felt great."

He looked directly at Sam as he said that. "I remember," she said.

"Yeah, well, I did a super fast job on the computer that night and we chatted for a while afterwards. After that, he would offer me a pill when I was over there, really kind of forcing it on me. I accepted, even though it made me uncomfortable to think about the consequences. So I didn't think much. I'd heard, like I guess everyone had, that there was more meth in town. He never suggested that I take more, and I figured that just taking one pill wasn't such a crime. The money he paid me for the computer work was a lot of cash, so I didn't want to stop working for him. He had me doing backups onto external drives every week. Any idiot can do that, but I liked the money."

"When was this?" Lauren asked.

"About the time the Dog Place got started," Ryan said.

He stirred in the chair. "Several weeks ago, I was kind of panicked when Paul Johnson asked me to stop by his office. Turns out that the police suspected that Mike was dealing. I hadn't had any idea, but Paul said that it even seemed like Mike might have come back to Silvermine and set up the dog training as a front for selling. He said it almost like a joke, you know how Paul can do that, and I didn't really know what to think. I was sweating hard, knowing that three strikes for me would mean serious time and guessing he might have an idea about the pills I'd accepted."

"The detective who was in Paul's office with us wondered aloud if I would be clean if I took a drug test. I knew I wouldn't be, but I wasn't going to admit anything, so I just sat there and looked at them. Paul told me how his brother back in D. C. had been murdered by someone high on meth, and what dangerous stuff it was. I nodded, I knew it was.

"The detective asked me if I'd be willing to help the police a little bit... It wouldn't be much work, but it would help them to collect evidence about Mike and about the people who were supplying him. I asked if I could think about it and he said of course. So I went home and thought hard. It would keep me working with Mike but without being able to enjoy the pills.

What if Mike threatened to blackmail me, since I had two strikes and a lot of people knew that? I knew him well enough by then to know that he wouldn't hesitate to play hardball to get what he wanted. Frankly, I decided that the money I was making there wasn't worth the risk, and I went back to Paul's office to tell him and the other guy that."

Ryan looked out the window a moment. Lauren had noticed that he had been keeping his voice low.

"They said they would not pressure me. But they did say that even a month more of my working on Mike's computers could make a real difference. I said I could do a month or so if I knew I'd be safe from prosecution if anything happened, and they said okay.

"So we set it up that I would keep working with Mike and would keep my eyes open. It seemed to me that they were keen to figure out who was supplying him more than anything. I figured I ought to be able to get some clues, and I started paying more attention. I'm sure that Mike didn't notice anything different in my actions, because there really wasn't anything. Well, except one thing, I cut back on accepting his little gifts. He didn't seem to care."

Justin said, "There I was in D.C., working my butt off, and this sleazebag..."

"Yeah," Lauren said. "Even right here, I was clueless."

Ryan said, "That reminds me, Lauren, of one thing I did. Remember how attentive that autistic kid Daniel is to what's going on around him? I knew him from when I'd work at the library at the same time he did. A few weeks ago, I asked him if he'd like a part-time job cleaning and stuff at the Dog Place, for good pay, and he took it. That morning that I came by the library and you were downstairs, I wasn't really there to work on the library computers but I had to give Daniel some supplies for the Dog Place before I went away for a few days. He wasn't hired for surveillance as such but I just knew he'd notice things."

Lauren said, "I wondered how you happened to know to come by the library back door that early in the morning. It kind of gave me the creeps."

"Sorry about that. Daniel had told me to come that way," Ryan said. He got up and stretched. "There's more I could tell you but it will have to wait. Gotta get home and take my turn with the kids."

"Thanks for coming by," Justin said. He stood up, and Lauren noticed that the two were the same height. Justin's body was muscular, where Ryan was very thin. The contrast spoke of their ways of life, she thought to herself. Justin put out his hand, Ryan shook it, walked out, and that was that.

TWENTY-NINE

Lauren, Justin, and Sam looked at each other after Ryan left. Lauren shrugged.

"Well, well, well," Sam said. "I never would have guessed that. Not Ryan's part, anyway. The Mike part isn't much of a surprise. Ryan stopped at a tantalizing point... because he had to go take care of the kids? Give me a break."

Lauren said, "I'm convinced now that he wasn't the person who attacked me, and I very much doubt that he killed Mike or attacked Marty. Betty's gut feeling has mine to go with it now."

Justin said, "I didn't hear anything that would totally preclude his having done the killing."

"You're ever the logical one, Justin. We'll learn more, and I have a feeling it will be pretty soon," Lauren said. "Say, Sam, I'm going to go back to work part-time tomorrow morning. I'm feeling better and Justin will drive me over at first."

"Cool," Sam said. "Well, I guess I'll go take care of my kids... dogs, that is. Business is already picking up over there, since word is out that I'm running it. Makes me feel good."

In the morning, Lauren was pleased to go back to work. She would spend a half-day in the office downstairs and see how that went. What with piles of things to do on her desk, and emails to wade through, her time went quickly.

Margaret Snow came by. They scheduled a board meeting to plan for the addition and went over a number of details. Margaret leaned back and said, "On a more personal note, Lauren, how did being attacked affect you?"

"You've heard about my NDE from Momo, right?"

"Just that you had one, we talked on the phone when she and Arnold were driving home from Mexico. I haven't seen her yet, though."

"They got home last night. I heard them pull in but it was around three so I didn't run over this morning for a greeting," Lauren said. "I'll see them this afternoon. To answer your question, I saw how a lot of my motivation as a librarian came from a core belief that the world needed me to improve it. I let go of that, somehow. I feel that I'm coming from a more peaceful place now. I'm just as committed to the library, maybe even more, but it's with a fuller heart. Do you follow me?"

"Sure," Margaret said. "I can tell that you are calmer. You've always had an edge that I don't feel today. I'm speaking of course as a friend, not in my official role!"

"Right," Lauren smiled. "Ditto. Would you like to have lunch one day and hear the NDE story?"

"Absolutely," Margaret said, whipping out her calendar.

By the time Justin came to pick her up, Lauren was more tired than she'd expected to be. They had a quick lunch at their favorite Cambodian place, and once home, she relaxed into a deep nap.

As soon as she woke, she went over to see Momo. Arnold's truck was gone, and Momo was in her studio alone, organizing her paintings. Lauren immediately noticed that there were far fewer than when they went to Mexico. "Looks like you did well," she said after their warm greetings.

Momo said, "I absolutely cleaned up! Any time I want an infusion of cash, I'll do another show there. And we had a great time. It was way more fun than you must have had here... how are you doing?"

"I went back to work this morning, and three hours wore me out. Overall, I'm doing great, feeling real different after the NDE. It was so good to see you then."

"Yes, I was glad to help. You look great."

Lauren looked down at her scabs and bruises.

"Not those," Momo said. "I mean with my inner vision. I also notice that you know who killed Mike and attacked you and the other woman."

"I do? I don't think so."

"Oh, it must not have quite bubbled up into the conscious layer of your mind just yet. When you hear who did it, I'm sure you'll have a moment of recognition."

"I'll tell you if I do," Lauren said. "Meanwhile, want to give me a clue?"

"No, you will know soon enough."

They chatted briefly about Momo's trip before Lauren headed back across the street, being careful to conserve her energy.

Justin said, "Ryan just called and he has more to tell you. I told him I've got to finish a report today but he can come on over right away and talk to you. I knew you wouldn't want to wait!"

"That's odd," Lauren said. "Momo just told me I knew who killed Mike even though I don't know that I know. When you said that, the spreadsheet I'd seen in that vision of Mike's computer came to my mind. It was a list of people he'd provided meth to, and there were only two names on it that I recognized. Ryan's was one..."

"Tell me everything at dinner... I've promised this report will be in this afternoon," Justin said, turning back to his work.

Lauren took Ryan into the kitchen to talk over coffee.

Ryan said. "Okay, I hear you suspected me, but I'll be able to clear my reputation with you."

"Good... Betty had a gut feeling it wasn't you."

"No wonder I liked her in school. The guy who killed Mike has admitted it and is in custody. He has no criminal record and says it was self-defense."

"Was he the one who attacked Tammi's sister and me?"

"Yes, he was panicking and trying to cover his tracks. He thought Tammi's sister was Tammi. He knew you were you, though."

"Who was it?"

"Billy, Jane's husband."

Lauren gasped. That was the other name she had recognized on the spreadsheet. She thought of how Jane had gone stiff and remote a couple of times lately. "Ryan, a few days ago Betty had an inner vision of you being furious at some guy wearing a plaid shirt, who was sitting in a chair, bent over in despair."

"She was spot on. Not one of my finer moments. It was over at their place, the night that he killed Mike, and he had just told me about it. I was angry that he did it and also angry that he told me and I'd have to be involved somehow going forward."

He grabbed his mug of coffee without really noticing it and let out a deep breath. "That idiot! I've been watching out for him all my life... we're cousins, you know."

"No, I don't have all the Silvermine genealogies memorized."

"Yeah, we are. I'm less than a year older but we were in different grades in school. Anyway, before the death he had been doing meth that he got from Mike. I was real worried about him. You probably know that Jane hated Mike's guts. That was because of the way he treated dogs at first but when he started supplying Billy with meth, Jane went ballistic. I swear she could have killed Mike herself. She didn't try any around the time I got busted for it—you know about that, right?"

Lauren nodded.

"So she was really upset. Malinda heard some of it from Jane when the kids played together. She did her best to calm Jane down and she thought it helped."

Ryan leaned back. "Billy is an idiot but he's in my family and we all tend to have street smarts. He went into a kind of cunning mode, where he began planning to steal the meth left in the Dog Place and disappear. He'd use some of the meth himself and sell the rest of it to get a nest egg to start life over.

Both Jane and I told him he should confess to the police but he couldn't think straight. You know he used the leg of lamb?"

Lauren nodded.

"It really was self defense, so far as I can tell. My best bet is that he went over there to pick up their little dog and maybe to score some meth and got into an argument with Mike. When Mike had been drinking, I steered clear of him... He could be real nasty. I bet that he went after Billy and that Billy hit him and ran out with the dog, before the girls got back from bowling."

Lauren said, "I guessed something like that but didn't know who. But then later, he was going to kill Tammi too?"

"Yeah. He let the dogs loose, thinking she'd come down to the facility to deal with it. He didn't really know her, and he mistook her sister for her. Then he was in even more of a panic. He knew the stories about you and those other murders and how brilliant you are, so he got it in his mind that he would have to do you in too. That's why he went to your place in the middle of the night. He had casually asked me if Justin was back and I'd told him what you told me, including about how easy it was to get in the greenhouse. Sorry about that." For the first time he looked directly at Lauren.

"I can't quite say it's okay, but at least I'm still here," Lauren said.

"Fair enough. I didn't tell him your library schedule. He just waited for you."

Lauren took a deep breath. "Anything else?"

"That's about it." Ryan got up to go, and then he said, "Oh, one more thing. That pink leash that you wondered about? It belonged to Jane's miniature poodle and Billy must have had it with him when he came after Jane's poodle and dropped it in the fray... Jane saw it and took it home. That gave her the idea of who would have killed Mike. She tossed it away someplace in the park on her way home. Another dog began playing with it in the park after that and somehow Paul found out. He remembered that you had mentioned it. That was part of how they got Billy."

"Man, I really wondered about that leash," Lauren said.

"Yeah, that was a good hit on your part. Remind me never to commit a murder anywhere around you."

"I'm done with sleuthing, Ryan, but skip murder anyway."

"Oh, I will. I'd better be a model citizen from now on."

"Yep," Lauren said, "You'd better be."

THIRTY

Justin and Lauren held a potluck on a beautiful Sunday afternoon. The 20 acre parcel they were going to develop for permaculture was right behind where his parents lived, and it already had a water spigot and some fencing, handy for letting dogs and children run loose. There was plenty of parking too. This was the first social event on the land.

The whole family was there: Betty and Don with little Rosie were there, of course. Justin and Don's parents were back from their vacation, and they just had to walk out their back door and across a field to get there. Momo came with Arnold, who was getting to be a fixture in the family. They had invited a few other people: Sam, Grace and Paul, Tammi and Tim, and Ryan with Malinda and their kids. Mickey was running and playing with Spunky, Rosie, and the guest children.

Justin gathered everyone together before they ate the food laid out on the makeshift tables covered with sheets. "We were already planning this as a Land Blessing," he said. "We didn't realize that we'd have so many reasons to thank all of you."

He squeezed Lauren tighter, and she squirmed a little. "Still sore, honey? Sorry. I just want to thank Sam for everything she did with Mickey... he's turning into a pretty civilized little beast. Thanks to Mickey for barking at the right times, particularly when there were the attempted break-ins at our house."

A murmur went through the group. "Oh, some of you don't know that part... Mickey alerted Lauren two nights in a row that someone was trying to get in, before I got back here. If he hadn't barked bloody murder, who knows if Lauren would be standing here now?"

"Paul, Grace, Ryan, Malinda, Tammi, Tim, you all had a part in what's been going on, and if you hadn't done what you did, again who knows what the outcome would have been? You've probably heard the chaos theory quote about how even a butterfly flapping its wings can change later events. Well, all of you did considerably more than a butterfly. And I bet you have worked up appetites. Let's eat!"

As they chatted over the sumptuous potluck meal, Grace told Lauren, "We have a new mystery going on at the library. There's a mousy elderly woman who always wears gray. She's been stealing fiction every week, including those new Agatha Christies you ordered."

"Too bad, but you can't suck me in to handling it," Lauren grinned. "I'll leave that for someone else to deal with! I've learned my lesson about being a crusader."

Justin was explaining permaculture to anyone interested, the kids and dogs tumbled down in a pile, Tim whistled *What a Wonderful World*, and all was well.

A NOTE FROM THE AUTHOR

Dear reader,

If you would like to read more about Lauren and her family and friends in the fictitious little town of Silvermine, I've written two other novels in this series: *Dead in the Stacks* and *Bad Weather, Bad Man*.

Here is the blurb for *Dead in the Stacks*:

> The Silvermine Public Library had never had a dead body on the floor before. The body was that of library board member Mark Wagner, and it could have been a heart attack. But of course the possibility of murder came up. Who would have killed Mark? What about the many women he hit on, putting his big hands where they didn't belong? What about the many people who had suffered from his rapacious real estate deals? If you counted up who was annoyed at Mark, it would be hundreds or even thousands of people in Silvermine (pop. 10,000). If you counted up who might really have done it, well, there were several suspects.
>
> Some people were talking about the library director Lauren Long, but she had her hands full, trying to keep the momentum for a new library going forward while everyone's attention was on the death. There was her love life to keep going, too, and then someone tried to break into her house, more than once. Was she marked for murder? In this new story, the first of the Curious Librarian Cozy Mystery series, author and librarian Zana Hart weaves a tale that leaves red herrings all over the library.

And here's the blurb for *Bad Weather, Bad Man*:

> Lauren Long, library director in the charming town of

Silvermine, Colorado, welcomes homeless people to use the library. One is Billy, who sends email from the library's computers and warns Lauren about a bad man. When Billy is found dead in the forest, murder is suspected.

Billy's cousin Barb comes to town and puts on a wild party to celebrate his life. At the party, Lauren meets Ace, a radical and brilliant homeless man. Despite being warned, Lauren soon agrees to a request from Ace which could cost her dearly. She came to Silvermine because of her yearning for a sense of community, but it seems that she may have misjudged some people, including her boyfriend Justin. And nobody but Lauren seems to care who committed the killing.

When something completely unexpected happens on her thirtieth birthday, Lauren must deal with panic. When she learns an important secret, things begin to make sense. Eventually Barb reappears with astonishing news, and a future better than anyone imagined begins to unfold.

If you go to ZanaHart.com, you can find links directly to those books. And there's more there too! I write about my current projects and more.

Best wishes,
Zana

About the Author

Zana Hart is a librarian turned writer. With a Master's of Library Science from U.C. Berkeley, she worked in California, Oregon, and Colorado libraries, as a reference librarian, a children's librarian, a branch head, and a library director. She has served on the board of the Northern Saguache County Library District.

Besides her Silvermine books, she is the author of *Living with Llamas, Twelve Walks Around Olympia, Mexico with Heart*, and several websites, mostly written as Rosana Hart.